PRAISE FOR ANOKA

While I don't read much horror, the vibrancy of these stories immediately impressed me. The voice in these six stories is urgent, insistent, and unrelenting, and I couldn't put the book down until I'd finished each one.

— DAVID HESKA WANBLI
WEIDEN

Get this book. Stick it in your pocket, carry it around, and read it when you need a jolt. It'll get you where you need to be.

— THEODORE C. VAN ALST, JR.

The stories in *Anoka* are scary and funny and gruesome and fantastic but feel true. The short collection is filled with big ideas. Its stories make you think, make you not want to think about what you just read. The writing is sharp throughout. Pay attention to Cheyenne Arapaho author Shane Hawk, he's going to write great, horrible things.

— TOMMY ORANGE

# ANOKA

## A COLLECTION OF INDIGENOUS HORROR

### SHANE HAWK

Cover Illustrated by
### SEWERYN JASIŃSKI

BLACK HILLS
PRESS

SHANE HAWK

*To Tori*
*Forever and ever, babe*

*And to all MMIWG2S*
*Their crisis crushes my Indian heart*

We will be known forever by the tracks we leave.

— DAKOTA PROVERB

'Everyone must leave something behind when he dies,' my grandfather said. A child or a book or a painting or a house or a wall built or a pair of shoes made. Or a garden planted. Something your hand touched some way so your soul has somewhere to go when you die, and when people look at that tree or that flower you planted, you're there.

— RAY BRADBURY, FAHRENHEIT 451

# CONTENTS

## INTRODUCTION: WHY ANOKA?

Anoka is a small Minnesotan city near Minneapolis and St. Paul. Its population reaches just above 17,000 people. The name Anoka originated from the Dakota word *a-no-ka-tan-han*, which means "on both sides of the river."

The maternal side of my family has history in Minnesota, specifically in Hibbing. Though it's a distant state from where I grew up in Southern California, I've always felt a connection to the state. My grandma and mom often use Minnesotan slang, probably without knowing it.

Personally, I've never visited Anoka. I've been to the Twin Cities and smaller towns of Minnesota, but never Anoka. To be honest, I hadn't heard of Anoka before June 2020. How did it catch my eye? Well, my primary intention for a debut horror story collection was to write all the stories from one geographic location. No, this isn't a new and exciting concept. The work of Stephen King and Matthew M. Bartlett immediately comes to mind. But I've always liked the concept of weird, unexplainable phenomena wreaking havoc all in one place.

My research started in search for a perfect location as my collection's centerpiece. I googled around for days. I looked up haunted houses, hotels, graveyards, etc. Something rooted in real-life folklore intrigued me. History is my passion and whenever I can connect it to fiction, I get excited. I needed a lesser-known place with hauntings and the perfect dark Halloween vibe. A Google search led me to the "Halloween Capital of the World." My eyes widened. Did I happen upon a real-life Halloweentown? Scrolling through paragraphs of texts and image galleries, I became hooked.

In the early twentieth century, Anoka experienced some real troublemakers on the night of Halloween, specifically 1919. Cows roaming the streets, tipped over outhouses, and messed up windows caused the adults grief. The following year, civic leaders came together in September 1920 to figure out a way to keep young kids out of mischievous hijinks during the spooky holiday. They organized a Halloween committee which planned a parade down Main Street. The rest is history. This year marks their 100th year celebrating their annual Halloween parade, however, the global COVID-19 pandemic has cancelled festivities.

My dad is full-blooded Cheyenne & Arapaho (the U.S. government recognizes the two tribes as one). Half that blood is in my heart, making me stretched between two identities as my mom is of European descent, namely Italian and Finnish. Split down my spine, I'm one half Native American and one half White American. There are slurs for me, but I ignore them. Luckily today the slurs are rarely, if ever, a problem. The original meaning of Anoka's name (on both sides of the river) spoke to me as a mixed-race Indian.

Identity is a key theme both in Indian life and in this collection. When I say identity, I'm referring to how one identifies themselves culturally, through language, and as a nation. It's something constantly on my mind throughout adulthood.

The two major Indian tribes in geographic

proximity to Anoka, Minnesota are the Ojibwe and the Dakota. In this book, the characters are mostly Dakota, though the Ojibwe and Lakota nations are present. This choice was deliberate if only for consistency.

My research wasn't only concerning Anoka itself, but also the Dakota tribe. You may think all Indians know everything about each other, but we don't. Heck, I'm sure there are many who lack knowledge of their own tribe. History lost in the minds and words of passed away relatives. Every tribe has its own language, history, legends. There is some overlap between tribes, but many tribes are unique.

Despite the uniqueness of many tribes, all tribes share a history of slaughter, subjugation, and eradication. In these stories, my Dakota characters speak with a Dakota tongue, but their experiences and attitudes are almost universal for Indians. Yes, we may all look different and have different dialects, but my aim was to speak to all tribes. The Dakota were merely a conduit, and I mean that with nothing but absolute respect.

I learned just as much about Anoka as I did the Dakota. My historical depictions and claims are as accurate as possible. As a historian, I know the *winners* wrote much of history and their narratives pervade the historical record much more than that of *losers*. Some information I came across varied, especially translations of words and phrases. My best effort went toward accurate translations without destroying connotations.

My mom, grandma, and brother visited Anoka during the editing of this collection and brought me home many souvenirs from their Halloween store, Anoka Halloween. I could not be more thankful for their undying support.

This is my debut. *Anoka: A Collection of Indigenous Horror* is a project for all Natives. My only wish is for all Natives to flourish and find peace. Our shared history post-1492 is beyond troublesome, but we can continue to heal through stories and love.

## ABOUT THE STORY NOTES

Each short story in this collection is accompanied by a 'story note' which can be read in this book's back matter.

I'd recommend checking them out either after you complete each story or the entire collection as they contain potential spoiler material.

My story notes offer insight as to what inspired me to write each story, what I aimed for, and the importance of each one.

These stories use a number of differing terms to refer to the Indigenous people of the United States. I grew up with the term *Indian*. I understand the connection with a certain 'Mr. Columbus' and understand its rejection. I also recognize my brothers and sisters up in Canada who reject the use of *Native* and *Tribe*. But for me, these words are baked into my life, baked into me. I am an *Indian* and a *Native*. And I'm enrolled in the Cheyenne and Arapaho *Tribes*.

Additionally, some derogatory terms for Indians appear in my collection. However, I made an effort to ensure readers understand they are offensive without being ham-fisted.

At the same time, linguistic reclamation has my full support. My Black, Hotep, and ADOS brothers choose whether or not to reclaim the N-word as their own. Not to erase the word's history, but to disable its future potential to cause harm. Folks in the past used the N-word for Indians as well, by placing 'swamp,' 'timber,' 'red,' or 'prairie' before the racial epithet. Some contemporary thinkers have voiced their opinion on the term Indian as similar to the N-word. I only want people to be free to self-identify and use language as they please.

# SOILBORNE

When we brought Roland into our home, he had a difficult time adjusting. For weeks, we tolerated the intense whimpering and writhing in his bassinet. The bags under my eyes sank heavy as if summoned by the vast, unnamed gods below. *Please, allow me one good night's rest.* When I couldn't take it anymore, she took the reins and consoled him. My wife would light scented candles and coo above him, her favorite old leather-bound book in hand. The baby mobile I constructed out of twigs, raven feathers, and jimson weed must have helped too.

"Good-morning-my-precious-little-
birdie," I singsonged to him. I set my coffee
mug down on the table and leaned forward,
hands on my knees. "Will you finally say your
first word, baby boy?" Roland sat back with
an aimless stare, still drowsy as daybreak
loomed. We sat him upright in the chair I
made from the black maple out back, planted
so many moons ago. *Time, where does it go?* In
Anoka, this question proved difficult to
answer.

Yawning, my wife held our baby close and
attempted a kiss atop his head. He squirmed
out of her embrace, wrinkling his nose and
squinting his cold, green marbles for eyes.
His knotted mouth twitched back and forth.
A silent, threatening tantrum that ended in a
rigid, warped smile. She muttered some
curses and jerked away to read a subsection
of The Book, audible tension in her words.
After a moment of regaining her composure,
she turned back to us.

"Please, please, please," whispered my
beautiful wife, silver roots peeking out from
under her brunette dye. She set The Book
back down, crossed her fingers, and bit her
lip. I, too, hoped Roland's first words would
be the *right* words.

I pushed up his greasy, wiry hair to sit with the rest, thus revealing the swirled birthmark on his forehead. It pulsated and glowed a faint green. With pruning shears, I cut away at the gnarled baby roots which kept his jaw shut, his voice imprisoned. A high-pitched squeal emitted from deep inside his throat. It was ear-piercing, not dissimilar to a mandrake violently uprooted beneath a full moon. My wife dropped The Book, and we both covered our ears. The screeching ceased.

"Da-Dada," he said, lush soil spilling from his tiny, bleeding teeth. My wife retreated into herself, defeat flooding her face. She swiveled to me, sobbing. I let out a deep sigh as my wife sank deeper into me.

"I'm so sorry, turtledove. I thought he'd be the one. I'll grab the shovel," I said to coat her despair in some feigned warmth. "Back into the ground."

# WOUNDED

Sixteen years ago today, Philip murdered his sister. At least, that's what his conscience convinced him over the past decade and a half.

His guilt manifested as a visible, physical presence. It stood at the foot of his bed. It walked across every mirror. And sometimes it infiltrated his television while watching his favorite shows. It followed him everywhere.

Every day, Philip walked to Pippa's school to pick her up after the final bell, but one day he ignored this duty. His friend told him about a new liquor store with an easygoing owner. He didn't card any high school kids and gave them free rein to buy anything from his bottom shelf. Philip requested the cheapest available, the black-labeled whiskey bottle with gold lettering.

He and his friend drank well into the afternoon and passed out. Philip made it home, eventually, to his screaming mother asking where the hell Pippa was.

Turned out someone kidnapped her from the schoolyard. Investigators discovered her body six weeks later at Peninsula Point. After heavy rainfall, a jogger spotted Pippa's arm jutting out from the ground. Her killer buried her beneath the Green Ash Heritage Tree. The coroner stated her cause of death was strangulation, visible signs of struggle. The authorities never found the murderer. No evidence, no leads, no justice.

It destroyed his family, destroyed him.

She was twelve years old, and he was seventeen. After her death, Philip lost himself in a sea of whiskey; he drank every drop he could. College didn't matter anymore, no hope, no dreams. Minimum-wage jobs here and there as long as he could keep them.

He passed through his early twenties with glassy eyes. He thought the thin film coating his eyes shielded him from the real world, from consequences. He thought the carapace he created could eradicate the pain, but it only blotted it out in erratic, limited patches.

Along with the death of his sister, Philip

wanted to repress his early twenties. He spent a lot of time at a crime-ridden halfway house. He signed up thinking he was going to help himself, only to find out the manager wanted to help himself to Philip. The acrid stench of stale cigarettes clung to every surface. Pills, needles, scales, and bottles of alcohol covered the living room's glass coffee table.

He came and went from that house during those lost years. Whenever he got fired from a job, he wound up there. When his world weighed too heavy, and it often did, he tried to kill himself, but the manager always stopped it. He always whispered in Philip's ear that suicide was sinful and everything would be okay. The manager often told him how he didn't want to lose Philip, that he was important and he needed him.

Throughout these years, Philip pondered about his surname, Wounded. Would he remain wounded forever for his name's sake? Was it his fate to suffer?

The manager got him hooked on many things, but what spiked Philip's endorphins the most were pills. All kinds of pills. He and the manager signed an implicit contract with their actions. Philip lost track of how many times he had to visit the manager's bedroom or shower. He partook in survival sex before he knew the term for it. He often found himself in situations to which he never consented. His vices took over and left him in a fitful trance, weaving between nightmares and ecstasies.

DUST MOTES SWIRLED in thin strips of light. The shed smelled like old gasoline and lawn clippings. Philip fumbled underneath the cluttered workbench to grab his bottle of whiskey. He bought two new bottles every week and hid them below the bench. He wondered why he still hid the bottles; there was no one to hide it from anymore. Old habits die hard, he supposed. Culpability ran through his fingers, his arms, and down his chest. The way every sip stung his throat felt like a reminder, a warning, to stop. The sauce never agreed with his body, or his mind, but he couldn't help it. His eyes hung heavy on the gold lettering across its black label. A measured breath passed through his lips, reminiscent of a whistle. The water of life.

His paternal grandfather bequeathed him a mess of a shed, but he found solace among the scattered, aged things. At a quick glance, one could spot anything from rusted bikes to worm-eaten lawn ornaments. To think, his grandfather stood in this shed while witch hunts for commies consumed the world. Different times.

*No, Grandpa "John." I don't need your damned church. My holy spirits come in a bottle,* he thought. Near his death, his grandfather was incessant on salvation and told Philip to join the church. He hated pushy religious types. But he also hated smug atheists.

John wasn't his birth name; it was Chatan Wounded, a "Sioux" Lakota name. The Lakota and Dakota Indians stopped using the term *Sioux* as it came from a rival tribe and had a negative connotation. The French bastardization stemmed from a name the Ojibwe called them, which meant "like us unto the adders." Adders are Eurasian snakes. The term insinuated that the Dakota and Lakota were Indians similar to the Ojibwe until the European snakes slithered across the Atlantic. The term *Indian* itself was a whole other story.

His grandfather christened himself as John after absconding from his second wife. He joined the Oak Haven Church posthaste. He died not long after. Philip always wondered about Indians who sought comfort in the white man's god.

SIXTEEN YEARS. The number floated in and out of his head. His fists and gut tightened as he bit his bottom lip. He shook his head while trying to control his breathing, but his ears pounded. He smashed the bottle on the workbench and sent the table's contents flying with a swipe of his arms. Philip's frontal vein bulged as sweat dripped down and into his eyes and mixed with a smattering of tears. His chest heaved, nostrils flared. His immediate instinct was to drown the pain, make it go away. It was all he knew.

He frantically pawed underneath the workbench for the second bottle. His hand nudged something cold. He jerked his hand back. He crouched down and gawked at what he had touched. It was a leather-bound book strapped to the rear of the bench, a perfect hiding place. Why the hell did it feel like an ice cube? Why was a secret book strapped underneath the table? Grandpa Chatan wasn't much of a reader. He reached for it as his cheek pressed against the table's edge.

He stood and tossed the book onto the

bench. Though he only held it for a split second, his fingers had pins and needles. Small flakes of ice covered the book as if it had been sitting in his freezer next to the venison all winter. With his gingham sleeve, he wiped away the ice. A layer of grime caked the cover. He grabbed a rag to clean it up, which revealed a large star symbol. It wasn't a pentagram, a symbol often mistaken for sinister things, but it had six points. Philip couldn't help but open it.

He observed its gold-edged pages and at that moment noticed his hand was bleeding. Pain ran through his forearm. The broken glass must have lacerated his hand, and adrenaline masked the pain. Philip wrapped his hand with the rag to stop the bleeding. As his blood soaked into the pages, the ice remaining on the back of the book melted.

Philip experienced oddities in his life, but nothing like this book. As he rubbed his temples, chopped up memories broke into his mind's eye. His grandfather's second wife, Mae, studied anomalous subjects like clairvoyance and hypnosis. Grandpa Chatan feigned heartburn whenever Philip mentioned her interests. Whenever this happened, Philip always sensed peculiar undercurrents. Though, he never pushed his grandfather out of respect.

He continued to thumb through the book as if on autopilot and noticed most of the text was in Spanish. Philip raised an eyebrow when he found English marginalia lining several pages. It was a distant, more formal English.

He came across a dog-eared page.

## HECHIZOS DE MUERTE

Spanish skills were but a faraway high school memory. He seldom practiced after graduating, but he remembered *muerte* meant dead or death. One entry was a bulleted list accompanied by numerals. A recipe? On the bottom right, someone scrawled **KILL KILL KILL** in red ink. Not wanting to read any more of it, he snapped the book shut.

AFTER SETTING IT DOWN, Philip walked into his grandfather's home. The living room was busy. A green loveseat adorned with a brown and black Pendleton blanket sat against the main wall. A wooden entertainment center was the main focus of the room. His grandfather's favorite westerns on VHS tape lined the shelves.

The fireplace sat neglected on the adjacent wall. Above the mantle hung a framed painting of George Catlin's *Scalp Dance, Sioux*. As a kid, he spent many hours staring into it.

His grandfather explained the artist's infatuation with Indians. He spent most of his career painting Indian affairs. Some tribes used to perform scalp dances, or post-battle celebrations. Male warriors collected scalps atop decorated poles and danced around a fire. As a kid, scalping terrified Philip. He fell victim to angry settlers and bounty hunters scalping him in nightmares.

Grandpa Chatan always talked about the forever war between "us and them." Indians were *us* and *them* constituted anyone oppressing Indians throughout time. He said in early America it was a mixture of the English, French, Spanish, and others. Philip had asked him about the warring Indian nations he read about in elementary school. He even shared drawings with him. His grandfather never wanted to speak about battles. He remembered him saying something like: *Those battles don't matter. What matters is the big picture, the war.* Philip caught himself staring off into the painting like he was twelve years old again.

PHILIP GRABBED the house phone attached to the kitchen wall and punched a series of digits.

"Hello?"

"Hey man, it's Philip. I need your help with something." Philip took the cordless phone out to the shed, opened the book.

"Lemme guess. You fell down in the shower again?"

"Asshole, I'm like four years older than you. No, but Angel, I found something weird in my grandfather's tool shed. Some weird book in Spanish with scribblings all over it. Can you, like, help me figure out what it says, what the book is for? You know my Spanish is garbage."

"Your Spanish is terrible? ¡No mames, güey!" exclaimed Angel, followed by a brief chuckle. "Yeah, yeah, man. Let me take a look at it. You hungry? I could use some grub; Michelle is out of town for the weekend. I don't wanna make another microwave quesadilla."

"I'm sorta in the mood for some pizza. Meat lover's?"

"I can never say no to pizza. How 'bout Pizza Boy in about twenty?"

"I'll be there, man! After, we can see who can score highest on Galaga."

They exchanged quick goodbyes and hung up.

PHILIP BEAT Angel to the pizza shop. Still sitting in his truck, he grabbed the book and re-examined the cover. He ran his thumb over the star symbol, felt the grooves. He appreciated its craftsmanship.

The book slammed open in his hands and the pages skittered across his lap until it slammed shut. His mouth gaped as the book vibrated on his leg and plumes of black smoke billowed up and filled the cab of his truck. There was a thickness developing in his throat and a light pressure in his chest cavity. Hurried whispers breached his ears, and he could have sworn he recognized at least one voice.

Philip blinked, and the blackness disappeared, no sound. The book lay undisturbed on the bench seat of his pickup. A loud rap on his driver-side window launched his heart into his throat.

"Looks like I'm..." Angel stopped himself short once Philip's head swiveled his way.

Bewilderment covered Philip's face like war paint. His eyes looked as if they were on the verge of popping out of their sockets. He turned to the book and then back to Angel with furrowed brows and pursed lips. Did Angel see the smoke? Did that just happen? Was he drugged somehow and hallucinating? As the questions swirled, Philip stuffed the book into his buffalo-hide satchel. He then shouldered its strap and stepped out of his truck.

"Aye, why were you lookin' like a freak-show back there?" asked Angel as they approached the restaurant's doors.

"Oh," began Philip before offering a chuckle, "Nothin' really. Your ugly face startled me is all." He gave a quick wink to Angel before holding the door open for him. "Booty before beauty."

"Wise ass," Angel said. They ordered their food, got their plastic order number, and sat at a rounded corner booth.

During their small talk, Philip couldn't

help but recap what had happened moments ago in his truck. He shifted into autopilot while Angel castigated their coworker Lazy Larry. He was a buffoon who often got paid the same amount they did for half of the effort. Angel often ranted about the day-to-day unjust realities they both faced as a Native and a Mexican. They were, after all, in ultra-white 1990s Minnesota. Philip overstayed his welcome inside his own head and Angel tapped his shoulder.

"Jesus, man. I'm trying to share my feelings here and you're off in wonderland?" Annoyed, Angel drew a sizable sip from his soda to give Philip room to respond.

"Sorry, my bad. I was listening, but I couldn't help thinking about Debbie when you mentioned the Marlow project in St. Paul." The lie slid off his tongue with mastery. Angel didn't question it, because Philip did often talk about Debbie. She was Philip's ex-wife who cheated on him while they were working on the Marlow project for a month. The cash-rich company contracting them offered room-and-board in St. Paul for the month. They were in a hurry to put up the building. Philip wasn't often the romantic type, but he wanted to surprise Debbie by coming home a few days early. Turned out she had different plans with a different man.

Angel regretted broaching the Debbie subject. It often led Philip down a path of misery, and in this case it did, as he forgot about the book for a moment. Dark thoughts raced through his mind. He remembered those nights he tortured himself in his apartment. He beat himself up, wondering where he went wrong. He thought he was the ideal partner: faithful, open, empathetic, and loving. How could a person do such a thing? She voiced no concerns about things not working between them. Thinking back, he noticed no nonverbal cues either.

Offer yourself, your life, your time, to another person for nine years and they laugh in your face. She spit on the grave of their marriage. A piece of his heart still lies in that cut of earth, that blood-soaked soil.

One of the teenage servers approached their booth, hot meat lover's pizza in hand. Without hesitation, Philip snatched a slice. He ate his feelings, pushed them back down alongside chewed up bits of pepperoni and sausage.

"Whoa, dude. I thought *I* was starving. Take it easy, fool," Angel said before stuffing

his own face. The sensations of greasy mozzarella and meats consumed them. Concerns
over ex-wives and entitled coworkers faded
into white noise.

"Hey, what about your book? The Spanish
one," said Angel as he wiped his face with six
napkins. "It's why we're meeting up, anyways.
You got it, right?"

With his mouth full, Philip lifted his
satchel from the ground and pulled out the
book. Its gilt-edged pages shimmered as he
pushed it across the table to Angel. He narrowed his eyes and looked up to Philip before
settling on the book.

"Nah, man. I meant the book we talked
about on the phone. Are you dumb today or
what, man? You're being weird, for real,"
Angel said.

Befuddled, Philip looked at the book. The
six-pointed star embellished the aging leather
cover.

"What are you talking about? This is it.
Open it up and check out the Spanish. I need
your help with some translating. Like I said,
there are some notes in English, but I wanna
know what the heck this thing is," Philip said.

"Hmm-kay." Angel shook his head, cleared
his throat, and began flipping through the

book. "This is dumb. You tryin' to gaslight me and on a Sunday? Take your dumb novel back." Angel gave the book a forceful shove toward Philip.

"Novel?"

"Stop, dude. This is getting annoying. I just wanna eat this pizza."

"How do you know it's a novel?" asked Philip. "You opened it for like five seconds."

"Alright," Angel said. He wiped his mouth once more and put on a more serious look. "Did you fall on your head today? What is up with you? This is David Foster Wallace's *Infinite Jest*." Angel smacked the cover with his forefinger.

Philip looked down and jumped in his seat, hand over his mouth.

"Yo, what the—are you okay? What's going on?" Angel asked.

"How—" Philip tried to gather words. *What is going on is right*, thought Philip. He stared at the front cover adorned with a bold, all-caps typeface and clouds scattered across a blue sky. First, the book blew out black smoke and now it was disguising itself as something else? Why *Infinite Jest*? Was the title a forewarning? Did it disguise itself as one of the most popular books this year to not arouse suspicion of passersby?

"Miss, can you come over here for a second?" asked Philip of a young, blonde server. Gesturing toward the book, Philip asked, "Have you read this book?" with the hope she would become confused and see the actual book for what it was.

"My boyfriend adores that book. He's reading it right now for one of his classes. He honestly, like, won't stop talking about it. It's super embarrassing."

*Shit. She sees the pretend book, too.*

Philip offered the girl feigned interest until she took the hint and left. Philip ran both of his hands through his black, tousled hair, pulling his facial expression up with it. His skin snapped back down into a look of irritated confusion.

Angel, not knowing what to do with his deranged friend, offered to grab a to-go box for the leftover pizza.

"Not sure what's up with you, but this is all too weird for me, man. I'm gonna head home and get to bed early. Early to bed, early to rise. Too much to do tomorrow!"

Philip dreaded the thought of going home alone with this hellish book. No one to come home to. Should he leave it somewhere? What was he going to do with it? Why did his grandfather keep it in the tool shed? Yet again, questions filled his brain to the brim.

He apologized to Angel for ruining their hang and blamed it on a lack of sleep. They agreed to see each other at work the next morning, bright and early.

*YOU VILE PIECE OF EXCREMENT. You are pathetic. I pity your futile existence. You bear no children. You have no partner. You go to work every day as a slave, a slave to the fruits of your labor. You spend your money on what? On things that bring you happiness? Things that fill that void in the center of your chest? You drink yourself stupid and watch the world turn. When was the last time you offered anything of value to the world? You mope around in the privacy of your home about your job, your ex-wife, your stupid guilt. You do nothing to improve it. You wallow in it.*

*At least, you are not a vain creature. You do not share your pity party with others, and you do not beg for compliments where you can. You are all alone, isolated in your own filth. Go to work, go home, go to sleep, repeat. Why? This plane of existence is hollow. Everyone pretends to be beautiful, unique, witty, or even valuable.*

*You lifted me from my slumber in that shed. You are not my rightful owner, and I am now tethered to you because you bled into me. But there is a way to sever this connection. There is a way to become separated, but you must perform the task by your own hand. All I can do is persuade and provoke the emotions. Kill yourself or I will haunt you as long as you live. I will ruin any relationship you hope to foster. I will torment you in ways you were not aware existed. When you wake, the choice is yours.*

BEFORE THE SUN breached the clouded sky, Philip was in the backyard in nothing but his pajama shorts. He held the pitchfork above his head and plunged it into the book. His clenched hands revealed angry spiders of blue veins. Mottled skin stretched across his pronounced cheekbones. Saliva collected in the corners of his mouth. His bloodshot eyes exuded a mania alien to him. He held the book down with his foot to yank the pitchfork out and skewered the book once more. Blood spurted in dark red ropes which coated the yellowed lawn. A caustic scent wafted toward Philip. From the punctures, frenzied earthworms wriggled and crawled out onto the crabgrass. As the worms convulsed, Philip pressed a fist against his mouth and puffed out his cheeks. He dry-heaved until some half-digested pizza spilled onto the lawn.

The worms extended and mushroomed into small humanoids covered in a translucent mucus. They caterwauled and quivered. Philip regained his composure and raised the pitchfork once more. As he motioned to thrust the metal prongs into one of the writhing beings, they all yelped in unison.

"Philip, no!" The voice was that of his ex-wife, Debbie. Once Philip recognized the voice, the creatures all morphed into her. They were all wearing the same outfit Debbie wore when Philip came home early that one day. Resembling a fish out of water, Philip gawped at them. He then fell and shuffled backward with hurried hands and feet.

"No, no, no. Get out of my head!" Philip grabbed the shovel and continued with his original plan. He used the shovel to stand up and swung its blade down onto one of the Debbie-like creatures. It emitted a brief squeal. Lifting back the shovel revealed a pile of salmon-colored guts and toothpick-sized bones. The mound of guts fizzed and popped like a thick soup well beyond its boiling point. The other creatures vanished. Soon thereafter, the pink pulp vanished too.

Philip struggled to catch his breath with hands on his knees and a collapsed posture. His head swung over to the book, thick blood still seeping out of the holes. He scowled, huffed and puffed, and screamed as he ran at the book. He picked it up and threw it into the hole he dug earlier.

Shovelfuls of dirt blanketed the book. Before the next shovelful, he saw something else in that hole.

It was his little sister's face.

He threw the shovel and dropped to his knees, his hands in a frenzy to reveal more of his sister's face. His body was tense, chest filling with pressure; his esophagus tightened. He sent soil flying out of the hole. The pink shirt she wore that ultimate day unveiled itself. Dirt met his tears and mixed; he struggled to squint through grime-caked eyelids. Spittle escaped his lips. Jump-cut memories of that day flashed behind his eyes as he dug.

"Pippa, Pippa!"

She had closed eyes, pallid skin. He dug

around her to the point her chest became un-covered from the earth. With his hands under her armpits, he pulled her from that damnable grave. He heaved her over and laid her with care onto the grass. He pushed a lock of her hair over to the side with trem-bling hands.

"You were such a beautiful girl. I can't—I'm sorry. So, so sorry." Philip held a pained stare as his lips quivered. Spit and mucus hung in thick strands above her body. "You deserved the world. You were so young." He clenched his fists and punched his head. First, with one hand, and then with both, harder and harder. In the past, he chose self-inflicted pain to relieve the guilt, to pummel away his anguish.

He wiped away the tears and snot and leaned down, his arms wrapped around Pippa for a last hug.

"I love you with all my heart, Pippa."

During the embrace, Philip sensed her head turning towards his face.

"I thought you loved me, too."

The voice was deep, masculine.

Philip jerked back with physical aversion. Before him lay a man, one whom he recog-nized. He was spindly with long brown hair, blue eyes, and an unkempt beard. His shirt-less body revealed many tattoos and scars; track marks lined his arms. His jaundiced eyes focused on Philip as he stumbled away from the man with urgency and kept his distance.

"Oh, come on, Pillhead. Come closer."

"Don't call me that. I'm fine right here." He gritted his teeth. He seethed in anger because his closure with his sister abruptly ended, even if it was all a mind trick by the book. He was once again existing without Pippa. The missing puzzle piece in his chest ripped away once more.

The man rose and patted dirt off his pant legs. He took several steps toward Philip as Philip cringed at the man's new proximity.

"You're a stupid book. A cursed book of a witch or something, I don't know. You don't exist. You are just in my head!"

"Why are you calling me a book? Any-way, we had such a rich history, don't you think? So many sleepless nights, so much fun, the ecstasy, the love, the pain." The spindly man bit the side of his finger to draw blood. He kept the wound to his mouth and drank in from the punctured skin.

Despite resistance, images of their shared past flooded Philip's mind.

"Why am I seeing you? Why are you here now? Why did you take me away from my sister?"

"I needed to tell you something." The man offered Philip an unhinged smile.

Philip gestured for him to continue.

"I choked your sister to death."

Philip returned a furrowed brow but rubbed it with his forefinger. He then scratched the back of his head.

"I'd been watching you in your teen years. Drove by your school many times."

Philip's eyes flickered.

"I wanted you all to myself but had to be patient. I needed to break you. I needed you to crawl to me. What better way than to choke your little sister until her neck snapped? Oh, it felt so good, that popping between my fingers. Extraordinary. The power I felt in my hands, in my bones. I took her life away. I took her from you."

Philip charged the man without hesitation, without letting the words sink in. The man went down with ease, though he got handsy on the ground. Philip was atop him with arms stretched out. His hands made a ring around his neck, knuckles whitening. He raised a fist and hammered it into his jawbone. How the man's face caved in like that of a rubber action figure startled Philip. He jumped up with horror, staggered backward, and tripped over the pitchfork. Philip twitched his head toward the pitchfork and grabbed it. He shoved the pitchfork's handle into the man's collapsed throat.

"How do you like it?" Philip's voice was hoarse and cracking; a panic befell him. With all his might, he continued shoving the pitchfork's handle down the man's throat. His flailing hands scratched at Philip. He kept forcing it in until he heard a terminating crunch. The man's mangled windpipe became flattened to his pulverized cervical vertebra. He lay there lifeless. Philip ripped the pitchfork back out.

The man deflated. Philip retrieved his pocketknife from his pajama shorts, kneeled down, and began carving. When he separated the man's scalp from his head, Philip noticed a fetid, yellow goop filled his skull cavity. It offered a pungent stench which stung his nostrils and forced him to rise and step back. Philip lifted the scalp-less man into his arms and folded him like an Indian blanket. The odorous yellow goop slopped onto Philip's toes. With disdain, he threw the carcass back into that hole. For good measure, he spit into it.

Philip relished at the thought he had won. He beat that infernal book and didn't give in to its demand of suicide. He didn't give in to its trickery. He packed down the dirt to be level and tossed the patch of grass back on top. He wiped his brows, looked up at the sun, and let out a sigh. After dragging the shovel and pitchfork back to the shed, he took a victory swig of his whiskey. Instead of hiding it back under the workbench, he brought the bottle into the house.

A muffled cackle permeated the earth and grew into maniacal laughter.

# ORANGE

Her voice. It still bounces between my ears before my head hits the paper-thin pillow. The sound of her voice comforts me as I close my eyes. But it's never enough to cure the insomnia—it was never enough when she was really here, either. But she still loved me, regardless, loved me with my tired eyes that watched too many black skies fade to blue without a wink of sleep. Her voice tells me everything is going to be okay, that it wasn't my fault—tells me I shouldn't look so grim on our anniversary. Some nights it feels like she's actually here with me, but I'm afraid to share that with Devon next time he visits.

Tried to get something—anything—done today. Read the same ratty paperback? No.

Do push-ups on the same cold floor? No. This bed is quicksand, or one of them finger traps. Try to pull myself out and I'll just get more stuck. No use. Better off watching the light play on the wall. What would she think if she saw me like this? The question repeats. Rattles off every corner of my skull, relentlessly. I sink further into the finger trap.

Before I got here, I searched for answers at the bottom of brown bottles. Aren't lucky folk supposed to discover messages in bottles? Never lucky, though. They banned me from Beaudreau's Pub for some time— branded me a troublemaker. Can't help it, forever thirsty and angry.

Couldn't help bloodying my knuckles either. Bill called me a "stupid Redman" one too many times. Can you blame me for going Geronimo on him? Those teeth I knocked out. Those teeth that gave me this here dimple below my wedding ring tattoo. I kept those teeth, root and all. One could consider me a collector. Bill didn't mind. He was sleeping in his own blood that night, his face painted pink and purple. After that, I started collecting more and more. Polished some clean, but kept most grubby and stained dark red. Loved the smell of pennies.

Strung some teeth together for a necklace, too. I hung it on the elk horns in my living room from when I used to hunt animals. It was alright; they deserved it. I earned those teeth.

IT'S A NEW DAY. Could force my eyes closed, but I'd only see a lukewarm red, the fluorescents soaking through. Gray. Shades of it, and black. All I seen last night and none of it from the back of my eyelids.

Green. I want to feel it in my pocket again. Been so long since I held a good-paying job. The only money in my name is from the tribe, oil and casino profits. But I make sure Devon gets those checks instead. Either way, my hands are good for more than just breaking the cheek bones of racists. Pops taught me fishing, welding, flint knapping, and how to rebuild carburetors. A goddamn pipe dream, me getting a job.

I try to remember how them black maple trees smelled—how their leaves felt crushed between my fingers. I miss that, but going outside ain't an option. It's tidy in here, and warm, but it ain't from the sun. Been a while since I faced the world, felt the sun on my face.

While I lie here, on this bed, it's like a lifeboat lost at sea. The dead silence bores into my brain until the air conditioning unit sputters, white noise like sloshing waves. Except lifeboats are for those trying to save themselves, their lives. Am I worth saving? Never prayed to a god before. Even in those lodges as a kid, I never connected to those dead spirits. I pretended to, though, to respect my elders. Could use a sweat right about now. In need of a cleanse, inside and out. Would put up a makeshift lodge. Just need a tarp, smoldering rocks, and some water. But nope, I can't do it.

I WAS ALWAYS ON EDGE. Too many conversations turned into arguments, then into fights. When my eyes saw red, when hot diesel coursed through these veins, nothing could stop me. Her voice stayed muffled. Locked up in the adobe crypt, in one of them ignored parts of my brain. The key was always missing during those nights of savagery.

WHEN HE WAS YOUNGER, I'd take Devon to Elm Creek Park. During the day, we'd fish at Hayden Lake, catch bass or bowfin. Flay them right then and there, grill up the filets on the public barbecues. After nightfall, we'd catch fireflies in mason jars. When he held them up close, the same bright flicker came out of his eyes, too.

I went to that lake without Devon sometimes. To do some business, take care of things. Return the natural order to Anoka; this is my land, after all. Anoka ain't a place I want them racists wandering around. And those mason jars? The fireflies were only temporary, catch and release, unlike the bowfin. We sometimes used to carve arrowheads from wood and obsidian, but my jars never held those. They held what I would call "marrowheads." Loved working with my hands.

I TRY to remember the taste of fry bread. My bud Eddie Navarro called 'em *sopapillas*. Whatever, man. My wife used to make fry bread so good. Drizzle that honey on it, the powdery sugar and all. When my anxiety built up, when I was losing it, she'd have it ready for me when I got home. She treated me better than I ever treated myself, you know? She was my lighthouse whenever I felt lost. Except lighthouses stop you from crashing into land. Why couldn't she stop me from crashing? The crash that tossed her through the windshield when I hit that tree. The crash that took her away from me for good. Not only her, but Devon's sister. She was in her round belly, too. Both gone. Taken from this world. Taken from us.

ALL I CAN DO IS TRY to sleep it off. Wait for her comforting words at night. Impossible, though, to get comfortable enough to reach a slumber in this orange getup. I hate orange.

# IMITATE

"Maybe I oughta stop reading you these creepy stories before bed," I said as I tousled Tate's bowl cut. "You get too scared." His eyes glistened with anxious anticipation.

"But dad, I think there really is something down there!" Tate held his red Pendleton blanket close to his chubby cheeks. His room was small, about ten by ten, and decorated by all his favorite things: action heroes, baseball players, comic books, you name it.

He was at that age that still demanded bedtime stories, but he was getting more curious about my knack for horror. For the past two weeks I'd read him stories that scared me as a kid. They scared me, but also excited me, made my mind race, and create different worlds.

"Okay, okay. I'll check for you. You say it's

under the bed?" I asked, chewing on my last bit of beef jerky. My arthritic knees were not forgiving as I made my way down to the laminate wood floor. I knocked over my reusable water bottle like the clumsy fool I am. Luckily, the cap was tight and none of the cucumber and electrolyte water mixture spilled out onto Tate's bedroom floor. That would've been yet another headache.

Shoes, missing socks, and toys riddled the space beneath his bed. I already knew I wouldn't find anything, so I pushed his stuff aside and acted like I was searching. "Nope, I don't see a soul!" I exclaimed as I held onto his bed to lift myself up to see Tate. My lower back was aching, but I didn't want to take any more of those damned pain meds.

"Dad, you barely checked! Can't you look longer and *really* check for the monster under my bed?" Tate asked with puppy-dog eyes. A heavy sigh left my lips and my shoulders sank.

"Sure, Tatey. Why not? I'll check again. Extra-good this time." Went back to my hands and knees, but this time I lay out onto my stomach. It had been a while since my last pushup and getting down quickly like that felt like a doozy. I was still facing the floor and noticed a board where the laminate was peeling. Crap, I knew I shouldn't have been a cheapskate with the goddamned flooring. The wife would never let me hear the end of it.

Looking up, I saw something new beneath the bed, some lump of mass. What in the world? A red blanket with the same patterns as Tate's blanket covered the thing. I lay there frozen as it rolled my way and unwrapped itself. It was my son. Almost a replica except his eyes; they were two smoldering charcoal briquettes with ash falling away. My own eyes must've resembled two harvest moons and my open jaw a cavern. I couldn't move. The boy was frightened and bit his lip the same way Tate had just a moment ago. He then moved his lips, but the words formed inside of my head. He told me something scary was above his mattress.

"Did you find anything?" Tate asked from atop his bed.

"Um, I don't kn—" I tried to say as I crept back up to look at my son, but he and his blanket vanished. *What the fuck?* I immediately shot back down to look beneath Tate's bed. Nothing.

"Goodnight, Daddy," Tate said from the

doorway, holding his red blanket and sucking on his thumb. He then closed the door. I scrambled to reach my feet, knees and lower back cracking as if I had driftwood for bones. Yelling, I swung the door open, but a dark, peaceful home said nothing back.

"Honey?" My wife, Meli, called out in confused worry. She jolted toward me and asked if everything was alright. The words wouldn't come out. I yanked her arm toward Tate's bedroom. Flicked the light switch. Tate was fast asleep.

"There was a clone, or something, of Tate underneath his bed just now!" I said, wiping sweat beads from my forehead. "He told me to look under his bed for a monster, you know, the scary bedtime stories. I knelt down and a carbon copy of Tate was under his bed, saying there was a monster on *top* of his bed." I realized I must've sounded like a goddamn madman after seeing the look on my wife's face.

"You using cactus again?" She asked as she leaned into me to examine my eyes. "Mm, dilated pupils, bloodshot whites. Please don't tell me—"

"No, no. I haven't in years. Scout's honor." My tongue-in-cheek mention of Boy Scouts didn't fit the tone of this conversation. I hated the Boy Scouts and their Order of the Arrow. Wasn't enough to steal our land, but the WASPs also tried to imitate our ceremonies, our regalia, and call it their own. My aging brain reminded me to return from my stupid mental tangent. My body tensed as I crossed my arms.

My wife raised an eyebrow, cocked her head, and rubbed her arm absently.

"If you say so. I assume you didn't get much sleep on the couch last night. Hopefully you get more shuteye tonight. I'm going to bed, Dak."

I opened my mouth to say something, but my tongue wouldn't cooperate. All I could do was watch her walk to our bedroom and click the door shut behind her. The couch would be my bed for the third night in a row. Before crashing, I peeked again into Tate's room. There he was, sound asleep beneath the glow-in-the-dark stars strewn across his ceiling.

THE SUNRISE PEEKED through the back patio door and filled the living room with its warm, soothing light. Well, soothing when you want to be awake. I regretted not sleeping on the other end to face west.

My wife was already off to work and didn't leave a note for the third morning. Couldn't blame her. I acknowledged my misstep, my mistake. Regret filled the crater in my chest, spilling off the sides, and I'd have to work extra hard to bandaid the situation. As soon as it could fade and be in our rearview, the sooner we could be a solid family again.

My unshaven face and unkempt hair glared back at me in the mirror next to the fridge. A reminder of how fucked I felt. Another wrinkle here, another gray hair there. More salt than pepper. I wondered what my dad would think of my choice of haircut. *Wow, Dakota. Trying to imitate the white man?* My hair was down to my ribs until my forties. After a while, I cut it all off to be more modern. But what was 'modern?' Was it erasing the richness of the past for the dullness of the future? A past filled with beautiful ornaments, character, and belonging traded for a future filled with grayscale details, imitations, and a different belonging? The thought of growing my hair out again became a serious consideration.

Grabbing the milk and Froot Loops, I

made Tate some of his typical breakfast. Yes, he could have done it himself, but I was already awake.

"Tate, breakfast! Come get it while it's hot!" I thought it was funny to make him think I slaved over some eggs, bacon, and toast when I just tossed some sugar-coated circles into a bowl of sugar-coated liquid.

Rubbing his eyes, Tate entered the kitchen in his Ninja Turtle pajamas, and offered a gigantic yawn. He then walked up to the counter and looked at the bowl of cereal.

"I don't like cereal, dad."

My expression was incredulous.

"You always eat this stuff, don't you?" I asked, rubbing my stubbled chin.

"I don't want Froot Loops. Can I have some of that?" Tate asked with his finger pointed in the coffee pot's direction.

"Coffee? You're nine!"

"Dad, I'm ten. I wanna try some coffee," Tate said as he pushed the cereal bowl toward me and crossed his arms.

Math calculations came into my brain. Sure, I was the idiot.

"Yeah, ten, I knew that. Just messing with you, son," I said as I ate a spoonful of Toucan Sam's colorful rings. "I mean, yeah, I could let you try a cup. It'll stunt your growth, though. Don't you wanna be tall like me someday?"

Heck, I needed some caffeine myself. My headache felt like someone was slowly turning a corkscrew between my eyes.

Water, grounds, flipped the switch.

If the caffeine made Tate crazy, that would be his teachers' problem. My wife changed her work schedule a week prior. She worked earlier to get home in time for Tate to come home on the bus. This meant I barely saw her as my shifts for Adam's Pest Control were from noon until around eight o'clock.

Poured the coffee into two mugs and slid one over to Tate.

"Cream, sugar?" I asked.

"No, Daddy. Just black."

It took me years to enjoy a fresh cup of joe with nothing added. This was too weird. I offered Tate a fake smile and narrowed my eyes as he sipped from his mug. After the first few test sips, he gulped the entire mug.

*This is way too hot, even for me. What is wrong with this kid?* I thought as only a half ounce of the scalding liquid entered my mouth at a time.

"That was good. So tasty. Can I have another cup, Dad?" Tate asked as he jingled his mug about as if asking for spare change downtown.

"Erm. Glad you liked it, Tate. But one cup is enough for a boy your size. And your age."

"Okay, fine. Do we have any peanut butter in the cupboard, Daddy?" Tate asked, a smile slowly stretching across his face.

My chest tingled, and I wondered if my lack of sleep was affecting my senses, molding the world before me into something unrecognizable.

"I'm sorry, Tate. Dad hasn't been sleeping too good. Did you say you wanted peanut butter?" I asked, rubbing the sleep from my eyes.

*Beep, beep.* Tate's school bus arrived. The microwave's green digital clock agreed with the time the bus driver, Mr. Delphan, arrived each morning. Time had passed like a flash. I could've sworn the clock read 5:33AM when I first entered the kitchen.

Shook my damn head as if to knock something loose and told Tate to run and put on his school uniform. My wallet was on the floor beside the couch, and I grabbed a five-dollar bill from it for Tate's lunch. As I looked up with the lunch money in hand, Tate was at the door, fully dressed and with combed hair.

How could he have done that? I kissed the top of his head, handed him the bill, and walked him outside.

"Have a great day, son. I'll see ya tonight!" Mr. Delphan shifted into drive despite Tate still walking back to an open seat. We exchanged our final waves goodbye.

I turned around and stared into the grass parallel to the cracked sidewalk while scratching my stubbled cheek. Tate was allergic to peanut butter.

WAS I LOSING IT? Does excessive use of cactus have long-term effects on the brain? I assumed the hallucinations were only temporary. The eeriness sent daddy longlegs down my arms. I spread my hands out on the kitchen's island as I leaned downward and concentrated on my breath. Dr. Langston showed me these exercises for when my world was crushing inward.

Dakota, my tribe. Became my name, too. Always hated the Anglo name my mom gave me, Jabin. Supposed to mean "perceptive" or something. Assumed my dad always hated it too because he loved calling me Dak. I think he loved me more when I drank, but not too sure.

Spiced rum and peyote riddled my past. The drink I took up from my father and enjoyed it as early as my second year of high school. Well, until I dropped out the following year. I joined a small group of Dakota men who suffered from sauce addiction and wanted to go on spiritual journeys to find themselves again, their purpose. Peyote was a Native's hallucinogen of choice. It was used to obtain 'enlightenment,' or have life-changing experiences with what they called greater spirits, entities.

My cucumber water went almost everywhere with me. Yeah, it was bitter, but I wanted to work on my health and fix a decade of dehydration. Work on it for Meli, for us. I drank rum like it was a fountain soda. Staying hydrated made me feel better overall, and I kicked the bottle down the stairway to hell. An actual battle won by an Indian? Something to celebrate.

However, it had been years since my last dosing of cactus. I still couldn't grasp how I tripped enough the previous night to visualize two Tates, or at least one imitation. The hallucination was so vivid, so real. Sure, I was sleep deprived. The couch had annoying, firm bars in between each cushion to keep its structure. Didn't help my chronic back pain. And I saw things in the past when I lacked sleep, but this?

And what the hell was up with Tate that next morning? Froot Loops were his favorite cereal. Coffee? Peanut butter? Maybe it was a subconscious rebellion against me and Meli's doomed marriage. Maybe he knew what I did and was acting out.

"THEY CALL IT A MISCHIEF," Rogers said. Sweat beads were crowding his hairless upper lip.

"Call what a mis-chief?" I asked as I covered my mouth with my forearm.

"A damned group of rats. You know, like a group of crows is a 'murder,' an army of frogs, a gaggle of geese," he responded with an appropriate air of intelligence. "Say, are you cool to handle this one yourself? We got double booked, and I've gotta get to the Henderson residence for squirrels in their attic. They said they'd tip me big under the table if I get it done fast."

"No problem, bud." I raised my hand toward his work truck to hint for him to leave. We often worked in teams, but it was okay. The job seemed easy. "Have fun with that," I chuckled, remembering the Hendersons as a crazy family. The head of the household had a screw or two loose. He offered me a half-ass salute, which made me laugh even more. Rogers was in the U.S. Army for some time, and I suspected his sense of decorum faded along with his respect for war. As he walked away, the large red and yellow logo for Adam's Pest Control on his coveralls bounced with each step.

I swigged my cucumber water and the back of my tongue picked up more bitterness than usual.

*Blegh.*

Maybe the rat nest's musky stench in the air penetrated my taste buds at that exact moment. The rats smelled like death despite the piss and shit I assumed lined the entire crawlspace.

After an initial inspection, I discovered two backfills and three burrows. I filled them with soil from the homeowner's failed garden. To remove the breeding nests, I first had to scare the rats with bright light because they're nocturnal. I twisted two high-beam lamps and threw them into the crawlspace. Nothing skittered. No sign of rats scurrying away.

Went back to my truck to place heavy-duty welding gloves on both of my hands. I figured if I crawled under that house and got ambushed by rats they'd have a hard time biting through the gloves. Slung my work sack over my shoulder, which carried traps, bait, and thick plastic baggies for critter corpses.

With body aches from my feet through my torso and up to my neck, I knelt down to enter the crawlspace. If I'd still been drinking, there's no way I'd be able to fit into that skinny stretch under the house with my gut. By this time, I'd sloughed off all excess weight.

For my protection, I also put on some safety glasses and a head covering. Cobwebs, random nails, and loosened splinters populated these tight spaces. Didn't want my coveralls to get too jacked up, so I used a small tarp under my chest to separate me from the grime.

My eyes caught small spirals swirling in the home's foundation. At that moment, I figured the heat was getting to me and I regretted not taking an extra swig of my cucumber water before crawling inward to avoid any dehydration. I also should have worn something to protect my nose from the awful smells. The stench was overwhelming and forced me to gag only minutes into the crawlspace.

An echoing screech pierced my ears and didn't sound too far off. The screech was atypical for the rats I'd exterminated in the past. Imaginary spiders once again crawled up my arms.

The lamps I tossed into the crawlspace covered much of the area, but left some corners dark. Those corners radiated the type of darkness so black your eyes see patterns and figures that aren't really there. Or were they? I saw more of those tiny spirals in one particular corner. Some spirals emitted a faint green light that grew stronger with my every movement.

With my limited space, I moved onto my back and fumbled in my pocket for my mini flashlight. Clicked the flashlight and tilted my head backward. My gaped mouth let out a shrill scream. I flipped back onto my stomach.

Convulsing. Bubbling. Popping. There

were seven, maybe eight, rats all melted to-gether. Their mouths opened in unison and another deep-toned screech infiltrated my eardrums. All three of my lights went out and a resonant humming filled my head. My body didn't thrash about and I didn't make for the exit. I lay there on my stomach in an all-consuming stupor.

The melted pile of half-dead rats gave off a fetid stench of death which strong-armed my nostrils. I dealt with rat carcasses often, but the stinging scent was overpowering. Remnants of my breakfast shot out of my throat with little effort. With bile coating my lips, a forced smile grew and my eyes became lost in the shifting spirals of various colors.

There was a large movement at the center of the rat pile. It was pulsating much more than before, but jutting out toward me. It wriggled and let out somber cries. A creature broke through the melted rats.

It was my son.

He was squeezing out of the sickly mess of rats. A jelly-like substance smeared across his face. Could only guess it was a mixture of the rats' innards. By the time he was halfway out of the rats, I scooted my body that much further to the exit. I wondered if my coworker sprayed chemical compounds in there before he left. Was I suffering brain damage and hallucinating? Dread flooded my veins and wormed its way into my brain, paralyzing me in a state pinned between fight or flight.

"Daddy. It hurts…" Tate said. Or the thing that looked like Tate. It was as if he was crawling through a glue trap I often set for rats. So slow. The colored spirals were dancing around him and in an instant, fell away, vanished. Steam came off his body like the morning coffee pot we shared.

Then his skin.

It was as if his old skin got caught on a nail, stretched out, and reached its ultimate point of tension before ripping away.

I remembered seeing a time-lapse video showing a tarantula leaving its old skin behind for a new set of furry feelers. It was simultaneously captivating and revolting. But this, this was only revolting. Dry heaves developed into more vomiting up my breakfast. The Tate-thing crawled through it, anyway.

With every move it made, I slid back an equal distance.

The new skin was an older Tate, a teenaged Tate. Still slim, but with long, dark hair and peach fuzz across his upper lip.

"Dad, just let me go. You can't save me." His voice was deeper, more pronounced. He coughed and black slime spilled from his mouth.

Quiet, angry curse words swam under my breath as I struggled to keep my distance and get the hell out of there.

I reached the entryway of the crawlspace and sprang to my feet, knee joints cracking like thunder. The moonless night startled me. I started this job around three o'clock. How long was I inside there? It felt like minutes. I watched the entryway for the Tate creature to follow. It didn't.

"Whoa, buddy! Easy there," Rogers warned as I spun around and almost knocked him over. "Did ya finish up the house?"

Though it was a brisk night, sweat seeped from my armpits and forehead. A quick swipe of my brow only got a small portion of it. I must have looked manic, though, I attempted my best to keep it cool.

"Yeah, yep. Caught about seven or eight rats. Pretty beat. Ready to go home."

"Well, you've gotta get your lights and equipment all packed up." Rogers pointed toward the crawlspace illuminated by jaundiced light.

Thanked Rogers and waved him off to have a good night.

Frayed nerves. An empty stomach. A throbbing migraine. Was time to get the hell home and unwind. Eat dinner and erase the day with some rest.

"WHAT DO YA WANNA DRINK?" I asked while face deep in the fridge.

"Apple juice," Tate said with marked enthusiasm.

"Apple ju—what?" I semi-closed the fridge door to question his choice. Was it happening again? Tate despised apple juice.

Our eyes met. He held a determined expression and gave a languid tilt to his head. There were those eyes again. Two burning discs of charcoal, this time twisting beneath creased brows. My neck hair stiffened as a chill swam up my spine.

"I said what I said, *Daddy*."

His articulate emphasis made me swallow a gulp of air. Down went reality and up came fantasy. This wasn't real. This wasn't real. This wasn't real.

"Say, Meli, what would you like to drink,

honey?" I called out, eyes still staring into the Tate-thing's scorched black discs. An awkward silence stilted the air. As I repeated myself, her voice rang out.

"Already got my wine. Come on, you two. Let's go." There was a clear tone of irritation on her tongue.

My body resembled a marble statue as I gazed into the hypnotic green swirls floating around the Tate-thing's face.

"What's taking you so long?" Meli asked.

His eyes shifting interrupted the mesmeric reverie. Those beautiful brown halos I cherished since the day he was born returned to his face.

"Let's eat, Dad," Tate said as he pulled my hand, leading me away from the fridge and toward the dining room table.

At the table, forks and knives sawed through meat, scraping against the plates. We always put a good helping of greens on Tate's plate to entice him to like vegetables. It was always a battle to get him to enjoy anything with nutrition. Tonight, he was eating the steamed broccoli without a complaint or shoving it to the side far away from the venison.

"I'm impressed, baby. Normally, you hate

broccoli!" Meli said with a smirk. She leaned in to tousle his hair and added, "My boy is growing up, he's changing."

Tate turned toward her and smiled while chewing. As Meli looked down at her plate for her next bite, Tate swung his head toward me. His innocent smile stretched out into a wide grin. The ends of his mouth almost reached the smoldering black circles, exposing his crooked baby teeth. A millipede poked out of his mouth, tiny legs churning about.

I slammed my palm on the table with so much force, my water bottle fell over.

"Goddammit! I'm sick of your shit!" Unchewed venison flung from my lips. "Who are you? What have you done with my son?" My heart was thumping, blood rushed through my arms and neck. The Tate-thing's eyes went back to normal, no millipede in sight. His face twisted into a shallow cry, then a wail.

"What the hell is wrong with you, Dak? Come here, honey." Meli reached out for the Tate-thing and it joined in her arms for a motherly embrace. She was hugging and consoling that... thing. Disgusting.

I opened and closed my mouth without a

word. My fingers repeatedly curled into fists. With trembling hands, I rubbed the back of my neck as if trying to get a stain out of it.

"I'm taking him to bed. Dak, you need to calm the fuc—Sorry, baby. Mommy doesn't mean to curse. Come on." As she got up to leave, the Tate-thing looked to me. It lifted its chin and covered its mouth to conceal a giggle. Its eyes were black holes, two collapsed stars pulling me into its event horizon. At that moment, all hope escaped me. The only thing I could sense was an impending doom. After I had shut it out for so long, the darkness was creeping back in again.

YARD WORK WAS ALWAYS TIRING. Hated digging ditches. Used to on the rez for pennies on the dollar. Thank the Wakan deities I escaped that place and settled down here in Anoka. The smell of moist earth comforted me. Reminded me of my mom. She'd make pottery from clay. Made beaded jewelry by hand, too, and sold it at the powwows. The monotony of yard work often drove my mind into those distant memories. Those ghosts.

The darkness bled back in, and thoughts

of her dying of diabetes plagued my mind. Those deep regrets of not visiting her, not calling. Was old enough to be out on my own, have my own problems. She always rubbed that worry stone for me, but I never returned the favor. I was a shit son. A shit husband.

Knew Meli went to her sister's house when I read her note that next morning. She didn't spell it out, but I knew. Said she couldn't handle me now, especially with everything involving that blonde woman. What we did. What I did. Was like carrying around a bison on my shoulders, the guilt.

My back could only break so much. Had weak knees and all. If a coroner splayed me open, right here, right now, he'd find minimal connective tissue. Where's all the sinew? You got bone against bone here, my friend. Yeah, yeah. Should've been healthier, should've stayed fit. All of life's 'should haves' and 'could haves' filling that guilt bison strapped to my shoulders.

My drifting mind allowed me to dig deeper and deeper and ignore all the energy I was using up. Swigged my water bottle; the electrolytes coated my esophagus and spread out to my limbs. A rejuvenation. I aimed for six feet.

FIRST THE BIRDSHOT, then the slug. Could fit more shells in there, but I only wanted two. Pumped my Mossberg to load the birdshot shell. Was the dangling dreamcatcher charm on my shotgun corny? Probably, yeah. But I knew my boomstick sent whatever was on the receiving end to a dream state somewhere. Most of the time it was a deer.

Oh, yeah, it was squirming alright. That was no son of mine. It cried and cried. I drove four stakes into the earth, one for each limb. Tied each down with a Palomar knot. Learned that one from the Scouts.

Wasn't in the mood to have perfect trigger discipline. Held the barrel between the thing's eyes, slid it down to its throat, then its torso. My finger teased us both by twitching.

Do it. Do it. Do it.

Big, black saucer eyes stared up at me. It writhed in anger as the shotgun barrel explored its alien body.

Planted my feet, firmed my shoulder, and released.

The tiny lead balls tore holes across its chest and face. The craters revealed a stringy black interior. The substance that made up its body composition was akin to a black, melted mozzarella. A collective of minuscule, sticky strands created a strong individual entity.

Those green spirals danced around its head. It was putting on a show. It was trying to distract me from what I set out to do.

Next was the slug shell.

The thing immediately went slack, all taut muscle fibers released.

I created a cavity within its chest cavity. It was beautiful. There was no heart, no vital organs blown to smithereens. Just a black mucus, thick as molasses. It oozed out of the hollowed basin. This was not desecration. This creation was far from holy, far from sacred. It was unknowable. An altered version of my son, Tate. It was demonic, or something of the sort.

Ripped out the stakes, which held it down to the loam soil, and tossed the knotted ropes aside. Does it deserve a proper burial like us? It was not of this world, yet here I was giving it a proper burial. Was I burying the idea of my son? This monster took him over and killed him. Was it my duty to remove him from this planet? To throw him into that hole and salt the earth? I'd banish this evil entity from my life.

Packed the earth down, a mixture of wet, heavy clay, and light topsoil. Threw in shovelfuls of deadened leaves from the black maples for good measure.

Sudden emotion inundated me like a monstrous tidal wave. I was heaving. Then I was whimpering. Then I leapt in anger and smashed the shovel on the burial mound. Smashed and smashed until my back gave out and rolled over sobbing.

Why? Why did it take my son? Fatherhood kept me going. It was one of the few things that made me get out of bed, to not wish for that darkness to take me.

The back patio door creaked.

Wiped my tears and the snot trailing down my nose.

It was Tate.

And he had those awful, black eyes.

"Killed the real son?" it asked.

The darkness emitting from his eyes drew me in. Swallowed me.

DEAD AMERICA

He paced his living room and beat his chest with an open palm, hoping to drum out some inspiration for his writing assignment.

The senior editor of *First American Magazine* solicited Chaska for a short fiction piece. The biannual magazine published work by Indigenous writers and artists. This specific call was for short genre work. They welcomed all genres. The editor wanted him to write about a contemporary issue within Indian Country and connect it to the past.

Chaska was an established writer in the Native community. He wrote captivating memoirs filled with outlandish and humorous premises—a few bestsellers and triple the number of awards. He kept them all on display in his office, but rarely made eye contact with them.

The deadline was fast approaching, and he had written only two sentences. Trash! If he were using a typewriter, he would have ripped the paper out of the platen, crumpled it, and tossed it in the garbage. He was furious.

Heads. Sails. Heads. Sails.

While pacing, Chaska flipped a modified Buffalo nickel to calm his nerves. His grandfather passed it down to him. Back in the day, those experiencing homelessness would sometimes alter Buffalo nickels. The Buffalo nickel was a popular choice because it was thick and offered a lot of flat space to work with. People called them *hobo nickels*.

Heads. Sails. Heads. Sails.

The front side of the nickel featured the side profile of a dead Indian chief, complete with a zombified skull and a full headdress. The word LIBERTY floated near his forehead. Three Spanish ships making landfall adorned the backside. Above the ships, the words IS DEAD spanned across the sky. When betting, flipping a coin offers someone a fifty-fifty chance of winning or losing. This nickel was a metaphor for what many felt was the predicament of Indian existence: fucked no matter which side the coin landed on.

Chaska's grandfather said his Lakota friend carved the nickel as a joke, but he cherished it. The friend wasn't technically homeless, but he felt that way because others on his rez didn't accept him and he faced racism everywhere else he turned. Other Lakota called him an *Iyeska*, which originally meant *translator*. It referred to Lakota who could speak both Lakota and English and translate for both sides. After a while, it became a slur reserved for any mixed-race Indian.

Chaska wrote like the wind on any given day, but here he couldn't find himself, his voice. No hope, no inspiration to push him along. Either way, he wished his grandfather would've been there to witness all his writing accomplishments. A small indie press published his first short story four months after his grandfather's funeral. But Indians try not to cry at funerals, they dance to celebrate. That proved more difficult with each subsequent family death.

He drummed harder. The chest drumming was partly to keep his mind focused, but also to stay awake. A month-long insomnia episode plagued him and coerced him to operate every day with minutes of sleep.

The dreamcatcher on his wall was a mere symbol. He thought only some Ojibwe still believed in it as a protective charm. Generations before him saw the Ojibwe as enemies for what they did, siding with the French. But he didn't care about any of that anymore. All Indians were his brothers and sisters.

Still, Chaska thought that apotropaic magic behind the Ojibwe's dreamcatcher legend was nonsense. He lacked faith, but for good reason. The Church committed genocide of Indigenous peoples across North America in the name of faith. And Chaska hoped that someday the Church would experience The Great Indian Reckoning.

But even if the powers were real, his dreamcatcher never protected him from the evil he experienced in recurring nightmares.

In those nightmares, spiders haunted him. It was only after these nightmares that Chaska developed arachnophobia. Chaska would find himself at the entrance of a cave, and curiosity led him inside every time. Though he wasn't in control of his own motions. He was a puppet, following a predetermined path. In the cave was a great spider. Three times the size of an average man. It slid down its sticky strand of spider silk to greet him with hundreds of glassy black eyes. It whispered into his mind.

"This is what you deserve," it hissed. The spider spun around on its web and laid eggs into his mouth. Despite his yelps, his rigid body took them all in. Hundreds of egg sacs entered his throat and crowded his stomach until his insides bulged. His eyes brimmed with tears.

The egg sacs burst in concert, sending sensations of pins and needles throughout his guts. They tickled and warmed his belly like a good helping of whiskey. But then came the pain. The spider offspring were liquefying his innards for their mother.

By this time, the mother spider reduced Chaska to a ragdoll, and he fell to the floor. The giant mother spider descended to meet the ground and crawled atop his body. It stretched out its upper four legs to appear dominant and daunting. Its fangs resembled twin pickaxes, and they jostled about before separating widely. A thick liquid oozed out of its mouth and resembled syrupy saliva. It came down in long strands and glazed his eyeballs. The mother arachnid then inserted its chelicerae into Chaska's slack-jawed mouth. It slurped his dissolved entrails with unhurried pacing.

Chaska's body withered into a dried fruit, pitted, a shell of his former self. With its legs swinging back and forth like machinery arms, the spider wrapped Chaska with its silk. The webbing always smelled cloying like cotton candy, though whenever some brushed against his tongue, the taste reminded him of horseradish.

His revulsion to the smell and taste was enough to lurch him out of sleep and onto his bedroom floor. He experienced that nightmare almost every night without fail. His conscious state was like the center lane on a three-lane highway, and he was behind a big wheeler weaving left and right over the lane, never able to continue in a straight path.

He got lost in recounting the nightmare and didn't notice how hard he was drumming his chest. With a final smack, he stopped himself and pulled off his shirt to examine the source of the stinging, revealing a reddened and raw chest. The agony of a migraine caught up with him and nearly brought him to his knees. He sat down to focus and wash the world away. Meditation proved impossible with the migraine, and Chaska cursed at the wall.

The condo's smoke detector spooked the hell out of him. He caught his breath, regained composure, and grabbed a Coca-Cola bottle from the dining room table. He was too lazy to grab the step stool from the garage and wanted the alarm to shut the hell up. Every beep was a knife into his ear and through his brain stem. In the hallway, he strained to reach the TEST/SILENCE button on the outside. It was what he'd press during any false alarm or when he burned his bison burgers. The bottle wavered just below the button, but finally aligned. *Click.*

To calm down and find his center, Chaska recited a prayer his grandfather made him memorize as a child:

Help me remain calm and strong in the face of all that comes toward me

I seek strength, not to be greater than my brother, but to fight my greatest enemy: myself

"THIS IS WHAT YOU DESERVE," it hissed. The spider spun around on its web and laid eggs into his mouth. One by one. It then spread its fangs. A translucent excretion dribbled down and onto his chest. Its mouth hole opened. The emitted screech was unbearable and foreign, yet familiar. This wasn't how the nightmare went. The screech bashed his ears with fury in a timed pattern. Unrelenting, he kicked the mother spider's abdomen and his foot shot through with ease, as if kicking a pumpkin. Millions of baby spiders rained down his leg and onto the floor. The black mass consumed him, and they trespassed his every crevice.

He shuddered awake, sweating in his bed. The smoke detector was beeping, screeching like a wild elk. Chaska glared at his red digital clock, 3:33AM. He awakened at the same time every night, except the dream always finished and never altered like it just had.

He had to quiet that alarm as fast as possible. He clicked on his small flashlight he kept in his nightstand drawer. Then, he ran downstairs to the garage unit and grabbed the step stool before running back up. He kicked the legs out and steadied the stool beneath the loud-as-hell smoke detector. Pressing the

TEST/SILENCE button did nothing. He was too overwrought to deal with it. His fingers stabbed the button with increasing frustration.

"Ah, to hell with it," he grumbled, twisting the detector from the wall plate.

No battery.

He nearly toppled over from the step stool upon the realization that it was operating by its own accord. Chaska smashed his boot heel into the white plastic disc several times. He plugged the sink's drain to allow water to pool enough to drown it. The beeping never ceased. Chaska let out a guttural roar with flared nostrils and a corded neck. Down the stairs, he went. The front door flung open as he sprinted through it. He chucked the smoke detector as far as he could into the foggy night.

His head throbbed as all the blood rushed away to his extremities. The migraine was back, and his right ear felt hot against the cool night wind. It was on the verge of popping, so he wiggled his jaw around to force it. It didn't offer a satisfying pop like usual, but it felt abnormal. A warm liquid dripped out from his right eardrum. Chaska wiped it with his forefinger and shined his flashlight on to his hand.

Blood. Dark blood.

At the sight of his red fingers, Chaska became lightheaded and hustled back into his condo and to the bathroom.

Bottle of hydrogen peroxide. Two cotton balls. A roll of toilet paper.

Chaska rubbed his ear with a few sheets of the paper, revealing knots of jellied blood. It coagulated quicker than he expected. How the hell did this happen? Did he hit his head in his sleep? Did he experience brain damage, and this was internal bleeding? Chaska's shoulder drooped and worry set in.

A sudden sharp pain knifed into his bloody ear. A clicking sound resonated throughout his brain.

Something was in there. It thrashed about. Chaska's eyes went wide, and he flailed his arms. He shook his head to loosen whatever snaked itself into his ear. No luck. He approached the mirror to stare into his ear canal through the side of his eye but saw nothing. Just a blood-encrusted earlobe.

He gathered his thoughts to focus on what could fish it out and settled on needle-nose pliers he had in the hallway cabinet. He unscrewed the peroxide's cap and dipped the pliers, a makeshift sterilization.

Facing the mirror, he steadied the pliers with both hands and drew them toward his bleeding ear. The pliers' jaws separated half an inch upon entry. The thing in his ear was still squirming around, which made Chaska squirm, too. Just getting the pliers up to his ear with any accuracy was a feat of its own.

The pliers must have nudged the creature, because it flailed inside his head with much more vigor than before. Chaska clamped the pliers down, catching the creature. Something between a screech and a buzzing sound reverberated through his skull. He yanked the pliers out, spilling the contents onto the sink's eggshell countertop.

His body fluids painted the white countertop with a mixture of maroon and gold.

Within that small pool of fluid was an insect leg, still twitching.

Chaska leaned in closer while frantically poking inside his ear as if it were waterlogged. There were fibers, or fine hairs, on the twitching leg. A spider?

He twisted his body and head for the mirror's best angle. His breathing became shallow, an icy wind blew through his veins, and all his hair follicles rose.

Seven legs jutted out from Chaska's ear canal, followed by a spider head caked in golden earwax and hair. Horns adorned the spider's head, resembling deer antlers.

After all the prodding, the spider crawled out and Chaska's instinct was to snatch it and crush it in his hand. He gripped it so tight blood left his fingers, causing a white, shaking fist. The adrenaline coursing through his arteries buried the immediate pain of the spider antlers lacerating his palm. A mixture of Dakota, Finnish, and Italian blood leached from the wound. His ancestors rarely occupied his mind during those days. The blood gave him pause.

The crushed spider guts gave off a pungent odor reminiscent of blue cheese. He hated blue cheese with a passion. An intense gag followed soon after, producing excess saliva in his mouth.

Ripping open the medicine cabinet, Chaska gathered ointment and a beige roll of bandage wrap with his clean left hand. The water flowed over his shaking hand, still trembling from the alarm and the horned spider in his ear. He wondered if it was real. And if so, why him?

Superstitions invaded Chaska's life from early on. He was always wary of that old folklore, those old tricks played by ghosts and whatever else. The thought of some entity placing a spell or curse on him forced his swallowing reflex, and he gulped down his fear. He regained focus on cleaning his cut.

HIS EARS RANG, and the sensation of an ache returned to his head. By now, Chaska was in the kitchen, having a frosty glass of water, rivulets of condensation running down its sides. The sun wouldn't be up for another few hours, a sight with which he grew familiar. Outside of the kitchen window, the brume leisurely whorled and crawled through the trees like battle-wounded spirits, clawing backward to retreat.

A crack rolled through the air. Distant thunder?

The faint sound morphed into a patterned stomping of feet, like galloping horses.

If old western movies taught Chaska anything, it was that Natives put their ear to the ground to hear bison or trains coming. His good ear came down to rest on the cold kitchen tile. The floor was rumbling and sent vibrations through Chaska's body.

Minnesota doesn't get earthquakes . . . Hell, he'd only heard about them in California on the news channel, never experienced one himself.

Opening the front door, Chaska sensed a thickness in the air. The trees to the right were still dense with rolling fog.

He lived on Cutter Street and across the street lay a beautiful open field. Only a few stars broke through the overcast night sky. If the night were clear, he would've been able to see Forest Hill Cemetery from his porch if he strained his eyes.

A bullfrog was calling in the distance. Then two. Then the smell of decay hit him. Something like rotten meat or sour milk assaulted his olfactory senses. The pounding continued and Chaska was unsure if it was his head aching or distant wild horses.

On the horizon, a patch of fog grew milky white, translucent. It expanded and drew nearer. Chaska squinted his eyes to make out the details.

Bison. Ghost-white bison.

The phantom stampede was relentless and on course to run Chaska right over. But he was dumbstruck. He stood there gawping and couldn't believe his eyes. The sound of their collective hooves was crashing, menacing. Once they got close enough, Chaska could see they were furless. Their hide, their muscle, their tendons stripped away, eaten. Pale ivory skeletons crunching and sawing back and forth, pushing forward.

With seconds to spare, Chaska snapped out of it, slammed his front door, and shot back to the floor. The herd of ghost bison charged through his door, over him, and through his house. Chaska lay on his back and witnessed the wispy white plasma rush over him like a wave of foam.

Rolling over to look back at the herd, Chaska spotted something else. Another ghost, though it was black and only outlined in the white atmosphere. A skeleton horse ridden by a skeleton man, bow and arrow thrust outward. As an arrow shot from the skeleton man's bow, the entire herd faded away. Gone.

His heart thudded against his ribcage. Too much. This was all too much for him. Chaska had been in the hospital recently for shortness of breath and chest tightness. Those symptoms were returning. Arthritis, heart disease, and diabetes tore through his blood-line, and he was no exception. His doctor said he'd die at fifty-five if he didn't change his eating habits. Type-2 diabetes was a threat, as was heart disease. The latter took his grand-father to the grave sooner than anyone thought possible.

Chaska felt damaged and expendable. It's what many Indians feel throughout their life. Was it thinking based on history or were ge-netics involved? He trailed off on self-re-flection.

*Are defeat and sadness in our blood? Do they pass on with every generation until we forget why we feel this way? Seems like we are a people des-tined to suffer.*

Everyone in his immediate family suffered from depression or post-traumatic stress dis-order at some point, both on his maternal and paternal side. Chaska's father committed suicide, and his mother died of a broken heart not long after. Or so they said. Other relatives passed away at young ages. Chaska was alone. The final Indian. He thought about the pills and the razor blades himself, but he never gave in. Never drank a drop of alcohol, either.

There came a rhythmic knocking on his front door. A familiar pattern.

*Who the hell is on my property at this hour?*

Another knock came, this time harder.

Chaska stood but hesitated. His revolver was across the house, tucked underneath his pillow.

*Shit.*

The third knock enticed him enough to check. He carefully pushed aside his peep-hole's shutter.

He gasped and withdrew from the door. This can't be happening. This can't be happening. A quick recollection of the night's events convinced him that, yes, it could very well be happening. He took in a deep breath before unbolting the lock and opening the door.

Steel-toed work boots. Dusty blue jeans. Discolored wife beater. Faded John Deere hat. A pack of Red Man chewing tobacco. His grandfather. He stood before him in the flesh. No translucent trick of the light akin to the bison herd. Just his grandfather.

"Want some?" his grandfather asked, stretching the Red Man out to Chaska's face.

He always found it funny he chewed a product named Red Man that used an Indian for the logo. He supposed it didn't matter.

*Any representation of us gave us significance, gave us weight. Made us not just some forgotten ghosts of American history.*

Chaska's heart was ready to burst, and for two different reasons. For one, seeing his late grandfather standing before him was both unimaginable and delightful. And for the second reason, he always warned Chaska of spirits returning as the living dead. Whether it was joking about George Romero's zombies, or familiar faces showing up at the door in the middle of the night, Chaska never knew.

"Zombie . . ." The word left Chaska's mouth before he realized, and his grandfather responded.

"No, not the living dead, my son. There is no doubt I am now part of the Greater Spirit."

Chaska never understood why his grandfather ditched his tribe's beliefs but chalked it up to his upbringing. Those church-run boarding schools fractured his identity—should have called them *breaking* schools.

"Why are you here?" asked Chaska with a hoarse voice, eyes fluttering to stay open.

"Stopped by to say hello, to send a message." His grandfather revealed his long, gray braided hair by taking off his John Deere hat, and held it with both hands below his waist.

"Message?"

"Short one, yes."

"About what exactly?"

"To stop spinning webs of lies."

*Webs? Did he know the spider in my dreams?*

"I do." His grandfather offered a slow nod, chin temporarily hiding within his wrinkled neck. "I know what's in your mind, too. I can read it. I can feel your fear, Chaska boy."

"Why does she haunt me every night?" Chaska asked. His head pounded, and his eyes struggled to remain open.

His grandfather opened his mouth to speak but closed it and cleared his throat. He took on a more serious tone.

"For fun. She's an entity from another realm, another place you can't reach here. She can enter your world, but you can't enter hers. Doesn't she tell you something every night?"

"Yeah, she tells me, 'This is what you deserve,' before filling my belly with egg sacs, consuming me, and wrapping me in her web." Chaska's face was incredulous. He couldn't believe he was relaying his recurring nightmare scenario to his dead relative.

"And what do you think she means by that?" His grandfather's eyes were glowing.

"I suppose what you said in your message. I spin a web of lies," Chaska said.

There was a silence between the two of them, save for the faint night sounds of crickets and frogs. His grandfather chewed some tobacco and sucked his teeth.

"You've stolen from souls not belonging to you or our family. You've exploited others for what? Awards? Money? You've survived all this time, ridden on the shoulders of those before you, like they were your personal slaves. Your memoirs are all fake. And we know it."

Chaska tried so hard to find the words. His bottom lip quivered, and his lungs involuntarily inhaled a gasp. His grandfather remained quiet and stared into Chaska's hopeless eyes.

His grandfather scratched his facial hair, which wasn't there a moment ago. Black stubble poked out from his pores. Chaska rapidly blinked to focus on his face, to stay awake. His grandfather stepped forward with one leg. Chaska looked down to see his work boot, but it wasn't there.

It was a spider leg covered in long, prickly hairs.

Chaska's head jerked up as goosebumps blanketed his skin and his muscles tensed.

Hundreds of glassy black eyes leered.

"Heads or sails?" it asked.

# TRANSFIGURED

Meat. Blood. Blood. Blood. Meat. Kill. Needed to feed my people, feed me. Hunted at night, vision was better.

Don't eat the bison. Don't eat the bison. Don't eat the bison. Turn away.

Heard screeching overhead, it navigated through the maples. The echoes bounced off the treetops. Then a song. Birds were asleep, though this sounded like a nightingale. An off-putting combination of chirping and trilling. Bats were the worst. My ears picked up every damn thing.

Not running as fast as before. Previous night a bear trap clamped my lower leg. Hated those metal Venus Flytraps.

Grew a few new teeth this week. They squeezed their way through the gums, pushed others aside. New teeth meant a new moon was on its way.

The pitter patter of rain hid many sounds, but this was unmistakable. Something broke a branch and crushed some dead leaves.

Extended my neck toward the treetops, cracked my mouth, and drew the night air into my lungs.

Wet deer.

Sprinted with breakneck speed, ignoring all signs of fatigue. So used to running on two legs, forgot I had two more to use. The chase was on, but I had the advantage of longer strides and human calculation.

Was on his tail, his stupid white tail, but my first grab at him missed, clawed through air. Shouldn't have cut my nails earlier that week. Always painted 'em black.

Next swipe put a hole through his backside. A bloody chunk of muscle and tendon lay in my fist, the ligament still attached to the buck. His legs locked, and he toppled over beneath a patch of firs. He was hefty, an impressive buck. Meant more meat for me and my people.

Tore through his backside some more, used my hands to force the hole wider and deeper. Must have severed his femoral artery on that back leg. Blood was gushing like a fountain. Annoying. Disassembled his hips and leg bones from the spine, a makeshift wishbone.

My snout picked up a scent that didn't belong, at least not this late at night. Heard a careful footstep and a faint click.

Another human.

Swung my head up, snarled. Spotted him maybe fifty yards from me. He had a dark complexion, long hair. Must have seen my eyeshine a little too bright, a little too yellow, because he shouldered his rifle strap, turned, and ran like hell. Flexing my diaphragm, I roared as loud as possible to make him wet himself. At least he'd have a story to tell. Pft, men.

USED to provide hunger-relief services up on the rez, the Mille Lacs Reservation, until settling down in Anoka. Was only about seventy miles either way, so visiting was never any trouble. Pained me to see fellow Natives so down on their luck. Their lot in life was rough. Yeah, they trucked on with a smile, but I knew what lay behind the lips and teeth.

Carved up the deer from the previous night on my stainless steel table. My hands returned to human, so my grip strength suffered. Used bone saws to separate the muscle. Stripped the carcass of its hide and always gave that to a male elder. He'd use the hide in various ways. Always gave the antlers to a female elder, too. She'd break it down for handmade jewelry: necklaces, beads, rings. One year she made me a custom coat rack. Was she unaware I didn't wear coats? It was endearing.

Divided the raw venison into weighed portions, eight ounces, and stored them in the freezer inside zippered plastic bags. People came with nothing and left with frozen deer steaks to feed themselves or their family—no payment needed.

The poverty got to me. Seeing them with so little and struggling day to day. Was doing 'my part,' but was it enough? Wished I could be a Native Robin Hood. Steal from the rich and give to the poor. The rich had so many loaves of bread they'd go moldy. Would they miss them?

The door's tiny bell jingled as it opened.

"Hey, Mr. Yellowtail. How are we today?" I said. He greeted me with a warm smile.

"Mm, same old, same old. You know how it go. Any meat today?" he asked. A look of hope seeped from his eyes.

"Just got in some venison. Gotta eight-ounce slab for ya," I said.

"My, my. Sweetest woman I ever seen." His smile was intoxicating, and he jumped with glee.

"Oh, stop it you. Doing what I can." *Woman*. There was that word again, floating in and out of my brain. Handed him a pack of the venison. "It hasn't had time to freeze yet. Get on home and pop it in the fridge or—" I stopped myself. Forgot, he didn't own a fridge. Was sure to offend him until he came back with a quick reply.

"No, no. Fine. Gonna cook this sucker up over my fire. Got a skillet with my name on it." He bowed his head and offered thanks before heading out the door.

"You enjoy that, Mr. Yellowtail! And Happy Halloween!"

ANOKA ALWAYS HELD a costume parade on Halloween night. Was what convinced me to move down here. A relative told me to check out the Anoka Halloween celebration the prior year, and it sealed the deal. They'd been doing it for like seventy years. Tradition, I liked that.

Kids would all dress up in their best Halloween costumes and march down Main Street, waving at all the joyous parents. After that, they'd go trick-or-treating. Wished I had something like that growing up. We didn't have much money; we were rolling stones, as they say. Going here, going there, traveling in our 1978 orange Pinto on winding U.S. interstate highways.

Always loved Halloween, though. The dark, the weird, the spooky. The concept of having at least one night a year to dress up and pretend to be someone or something else intrigued me. Halloween hooked me, even when I had nothing. Aside from the costumes and stuff, you didn't need much to celebrate, just your imagination and a good spirit. This year, I'd get my Halloween.

Was what I had a blessing or a curse? At first, it devastated me. Was sure it would devastate anybody. But now? Now, it felt like freedom. The witch who placed this lycanthropy spell on me was petty. Crossed her in such a minimal way and out came The Book.

Ridiculous. But by now I was over it. No harm, no foul. This was my life.

My body transitioned with the day. Beauty by sunrise, beast by sunset. Not to say I was a looker. Hated talking about my appearance. But at night, I reigned. Felt more alive as a brute, more free. With no one watching, I was free to be my true self, my true form.

Hated how rigid it was, either one or the other, could never be a combination of the two. Daylight dragged and I counted down the minutes. Couldn't wait to transform again.

WAS an hour until the moon rose when I locked up my little food bank. Headed home with pure excitement, tapped the steering wheel to the beat of one of my favorite Thompson Twins songs:

> She's a lonely woman...
> Then he comes home one night,
> She kills him with a knife.
> Now she's the one who's living in
> paradise.

Turning hurt every time, but it was getting easier. Most things are like that. The sky's transition to twilight prompted me to go to my backyard, to my shed. Only saw two stars puncture the early night sky before I bolted that door. Every change left a residual odor. Reminded me of burnt hair and a week-old animal corpse. Couldn't get rid of the smell with any spray from the store, so I stopped trying. Got used to it, anyway.

Messy. Always grotesque and messy. I remember the first time it happened. Couldn't believe the steaming pile of my body remnants sitting before me. But now it was time. A full moon ensured an easier transition. When the moon revealed its entire self, it revitalized my being. Felt younger, stronger, faster.

Crack. Pop. Sounds of stretching bones and ripping skin filled my shed. My hairy snout pushed through my face like that chest-burster in *Alien*. Eyeballs melted down. Wide shoulders burst out from my much smaller frame like a bloated mouse stuffed with gray maggots.

*Shit*. Forgot to take one of my rings off. The tension snapped it in half and it fell to the floor as my hands became elongated

paws. Enjoyed looking down to see my pedi-
cured toenails thicken into sharpened claws.
My big toes shriveled up and moved upward
on my hind paws to form dewclaws. After the
mucus my body produced for transition
dried up, I stood and stretched my renewed
limbs and back. In this form, my head almost
hit the shed's roof. Had to stoop through the
doorway.

Tossed my melted remains in my bonfire
pit. Was like a full skin bodysuit. Could've
sold 'em to Buffalo Bill types. Saw that movie
earlier that year. Was sympathetic for him in
some ways. Wouldn't hesitate to rip his face
off, though. Was time for the parade. I'd burn
my skin suit later.

THE RUM RIVER FROZE OVER. Had to crack
open the thin top layer of ice to float down-
stream. Couldn't imagine doing this in my
human body. With thick fur, it was still cold
as all hell. Took breaks here and there. It was
dark, but not enough for the city to turn on
the streetlamps.

River water ran down my coat as I hud-
dled underneath the Rum River Bridge.

Shook my fur out, but it wasn't enough to dry all the way. The parade's route began right above me on the bridge, so I was right where I needed to be.

Stared across the river at Windego Park, an old-ass amphitheater. They built it in the 1910s and took its name from the old Ojibwe legend. Their legend said Windegos were as tall as trees and were born whenever a human resorted to cannibalism to survive. Some Ojibwe claimed they had special powers to possess, too.

They weren't my tribe, but I believed that legend. Witches and werewolves were real. Why not Windegos? And isn't that what happened to the Donner Party out in California? Being so desperate for meat, for food. Could relate to that. Pitied any person with nothing to fall back on, enough to eat someone's heart out.

Enough time passed to dry my winter coat. Checked both sides of the bridge and chose the north bank to crawl up.

There were hundreds of attendees, both children and parents. The Halloween committee went all out. They strung orange lights between each lamp post, festooned street signs with orange and black garland, blasted

*Monster Mash* on PA speakers, and decorated the entire parade route with fake cobwebs. The scent of cotton candy and caramel apples floated through the air. It was magical. Mummies, goblins, witches, ghosts. Those kids had 'em all. Couldn't see behind their masks, but could only guess a grin stretched across their faces. A middle-aged dad with his daughter stepped up to me. The daughter's costume was Lydia from *Beetlejuice*.

"Uff-da! Pretty realistic costume you got there, mister." He cleared his throat after a moment-too-long stare. "Holy buckets, I'm sorry. Would you like a gingersnap cookie?" The man holding out a plate of cookies had thinning hair, a potbelly, and a heather-gray sweatshirt with a Batman logo across the chest. Tried my best to reply, as if I were Little Red inside the wolf's belly. Kept my jaw cracked open and didn't move it while talking.

"You betcha!" My reply must have satisfied him as he smiled, pulled his daughter in close, and placed a gingersnap into my open palm. He nodded and they continued on down Main Street.

Between each horde of kids was a Halloween float strapped atop a car, well, mostly flatbed trucks. They crept along the route, which was only about four blocks long.

Kids were dancing, flailing their arms, and shouting MONSTER MASH!

Then the snow came.

Couldn't ever remember it snowing so early. In fact, it was the coldest Halloween night I could remember. The snow was light at first, soft, puffy flakes floating down at random. Then the wind picked up and sent chills through our collective spine. Felt like the entire street shivered in unison. The main PA speaker ripped away from its post and left behind dangling cords. The Halloween music abruptly stopped.

This alarmed the crowd, but not enough for the parade to stop. A passionate committee member yelled out an apology and told everyone to keep moving. Walked alongside a float embellished with large jack-o'-lanterns, bats, and black cats, all made with a similar material as piñatas. For a moment, I wished this all could've been part of my childhood. A fleeting worm of envy swam through my blood.

That's when the symbol came. A large green swirl materialized and hovered over

Main Street. Was hypnotic. At least for the children.

Every single child stopped what they were doing and gazed into the green swirl, mesmerized. Many of the parents didn't notice until they stopped walking, looked back at their children, and craned their neck toward the sky.

The floats came to a halt, save for one. The last float operator was blasting Michael Jackson's *Thriller* on their tape deck and hadn't seen the green sky swirl. They didn't apply their brakes until they had already run over four people, crushing them beneath the huge snow tires. The driver jumped out of the vehicle and screamed, rushing over to the four trampled attendees.

The accident forced the adults to scramble toward the front of the float, temporarily ditching their children. One parent hopped into the driver's seat to shift the truck into neutral. He ran back out to the hood, yelled for help, and they pushed the truck back enough to reveal the bodies. A family of four: two young boys, and two parents.

Had nowhere to go, stuck in the crowd, and unsure what to do. Didn't know what the hell was going on with the green swirl. Contemplated running back home, up north, along the river.

The children let out a chorus of guttural caws.

One mother screamed. Her daughter was biting her ankle like a deranged dog. Saw her rip away her Achilles tendon.

Then another. And another.

Frenzied children filled the entire street, knocking over weak-kneed parents and consuming their flesh.

My jaw dropped as I watched a little girl dressed as a pirate chomping on her father's jugular veins like licorice. She looked up at me, smiling. The blood smeared across her face as though she drank from a punch bowl.

Saw a sobbing father punching and kicking at kids for his own survival. Was as though they operated on a hive mind. About ten of them teamed up to take the crying father down. Crept backward to hide behind a brick-walled building. The carnage was worse than any of my nighttime hunts. Felt ill, but my wolf body was incapable of vomiting.

The streets were fraught with cries and flesh-eating. Was like a train wreck, so horrible and saddening, but couldn't help but stare. My gut bottomed out as I watched them all.

The snow ripped down harder than ever. The snowfall slowly covered the dead bodies, coating them with white powder like a pastry chef.

After the last scream rang through the snowy sky, the kids gathered all the torn human flesh and packed it into their trick-or-treat bags and buckets. Stood there stupefied, watching these cute children, drenched in gore, place severed hands, heads, and feet, into their orange jack-o'-lantern buckets without a misstep.

Noticed the children created a single-file line and marched the opposite way of the parade route. They walked toward the beginning near the bridge. Snuck alongside the floats, just out their view, to see where they were going.

The line of children walked down the slight hill, arms outstretched with their pound of flesh, toward the Rum River. They walked toward a giant tree planted on the other side of the river.

Though, it wasn't a tree.

Its arms and legs extended, and it walked into the icy black river.

It held my stare with its glowing red eyes and let out a bellow of rage.

It was the deer hunter.

## SOILBORNE

Horror surrounding birth and babies is effective. Carrying a child and giving birth has to be one of life's greatest highlights. Children are one of the most precious gifts we receive. Anything going wrong with either of these punches you in the gut. Hard. Stillbirths are devastating. Any loss of mother or child is world-ending. I came across a social media post where this couple could not conceive due to problems with both the mother's and father's biology. I wondered how heartbreaking it would be to want a child and being denied on a biological level. With *Soilborne*, I aimed to creep everyone the hell out in the final act. Everything before that is uplifting, or at least innocent and charming. It's not until the reader knows he has an alien-feeling birthmark that something is truly off. Alarm bells! The final revelation should shock anyone with a heart. I say that lovingly!

## WOUNDED

Ah, spell books, guilt, addiction, broken relationships, missing siblings, and revenge. I'd say that's a decent combination for a story with lots of emotional turns. I said a lot with this story and delved into many issues plaguing Indian life, both past and present. Alcoholism affects many families but is widespread in Indian Country. It leads to other health ailments and opens families up to both mental and physical abuse. My late stepfather inspired some of this story. He suffered from alcoholism until his death in 2016. The grandfather briefly mentioned in the story is Chatan Wounded, which translates to Wounded Hawk. No family likes to delve into its checkered history, so I won't speak ill of the dead. Like any man taking the new title of stepdad, he had a complicated road ahead of him. He was in my life for sixteen years and had quite the impact, good and bad. I'll miss him. With this story, I also wanted to pay respect to the crisis of missing and murdered Indigenous women and girls (MMIWG) and bring it to my readers' attention. It's a gigantic problem that requires awareness. We have to do what we can. Where do we go from here?

## ORANGE

*Orange* was the second story in which I took a stab at flash fiction. Flash fiction is a different ball game than other short fiction. It may seem easier on the surface, but it forces writers to cut away all fat with a machete. Flash fiction is lean and mean. Do you know how hard it is to elicit emotional reactions from people with so few words *and* include a foreshadowed twist?! I worked more on *Orange* and *Soilborne* than any other story in this collection. A mixture of things inspired this story: my personal battle with depression, my dad's cool personality, racism toward Indians, and Showtime's *Dexter*. With *Orange*, I aimed to showcase how I experienced depression. I lost interest in many things, didn't know what to do with myself, and forced myself to reminisce to the ever-fleeting "good ol' days,"

the halcyon days of yore. The reader is unaware of the main character's situation until
they read the last sentence. A quick re-read
helps to fill the gaps, and everything makes
sense. I entertained myself by creating my
very own Indian *Dexter*. The TV show character, from what I watched, always killed the
bad guys. I wanted to show what could
happen if a person, blinded by alcohol, ha-
tred, and despair, walked down a destructive
path. The reader should question the validity
or the moral implication of his killings and
ponder whether the reasons are justifiable.
It's supposed to unsettle.

## IMITATE

The title of this story is on the nose, (IMI-
being a palindrome, or a mirrored prefix, and
-TATE being, well, the boy's name) but on the
nose is fun sometimes. I drew inspiration
from Kealan Patrick Burke's novella, *Sour
Candy*, which freaked me the hell out. I also
injected 1980s horror movie nastiness, with
all their grotesque practical effects, into this
story. And maybe a dash of *Pet Sematary* if it
were written by someone even more messed
up than Stephen King (not saying I am, for
legal reasons). *Imitate* is a story about a father

with a fucked up history with drugs trying his best to love his wife and son. He stumbles and cheats on his wife, and it throws his world through a loop. He wants to be the best dad he can be, but it doesn't seem like it's in his cards. His son changes, first in minor ways and later in major and odd ways. The son's transformation is a metaphor for growing sons that may drift away from their father, either in actual proximity or in shared interests. The dad can't handle it besides everything else and finally acts. He completely loses it. Hopefully, the ending is surprising and revolting because that was my aim. Finding out that murdering your own child, and not some demonic clone, must flip a father's world inside out. Again, the murder and/or death of children is one of the most horrific things in the tangible human world. I used it as an exaggerated demonstration of a father's refusal to accept change. For those who don't know, I chose the wife's name to be Meli because it translates to bitter, an allusion to his cucumber water and their relationship. And yes, the Tate-thing was dropping mescaline powder in the father's water bottle.

**DEAD AMERICA**

This story was fun to write and my girl-friend told me it's my most well-written one. The title came from my dad. We were texting one day, and I sent him a picture of an altered half dollar coin I found on the internet. It had an Indian chief, but his face was a skull. I'm all about the morbid and weird and thought nothing of it, but my dad replied, "Dead America." I sat there and pondered his inter-pretation for a few minutes, and it lodged it-self in the back of my brain like a popcorn kernel between molars. The story itself is meta. While writing this collection, I came across "writer's block" despite all the ideas pinballing between my synapses. I did repeti-tive motions with my hands and paced around my house to trigger something, any-thing. My smoke detector went haywire, too. Drove me nuts. Also, spiders suck. No one likes them. If you say you do, you're a liar. Re-searching the movements and body composi-tion of spiders made me shiver. So did writing that sentence and revisiting that memory. *Yeah, yeah, so what? Spiders, I get it.* Well, I alluded to a popular Ojibwe legend about the Spider Woman and how it's con-nected to dreamcatchers. In that legend, the

Spider Woman is a protector of children. In my story, she's a literal spider and makes Chaska pay for what he's done night after night. The guilt for stealing all of his memoir's stories is subconscious. He repressed all of it to feel a sense of belonging. Death haunted his family, and he was essentially the last one left. Concentrating on fame and fortune made him lose sight of his own story, his people's own past. He didn't have to steal other people's stories to make a living. He had plenty of material to work with right in front of him. And that visit from his "grandpa"... What do you think happened to him? What came next?

## TRANSFIGURED

I love werewolves, but they're no longer scary. They're so ubiquitous in pop culture to the point of being seen as harmless. The same has happened to zombies, mummies, (Were mummies ever frightening? *Under Wraps* was awesome.) witches, vampires, and other classic horror characters. My main vision for this collection was to include a story involving a werewolf, hence the cover art. The image on the front of this book is a traditionally terrifying werewolf because that's what everyone loves, including me. Because they aren't scary anymore, werewolves are more of a vehicle to tell other stories now. Think of Stephen Graham Jones's *Mongrels*. In my mind, the modern werewolf is a perfect allusion to some people in the queer community. My werewolf is genderfluid. They struggle with the transformation between biological woman and werewolf because of the strict adherence to one or the other depending on the sun and moon. They wish there could be a blending of the two, but the witch permanently set the spell this way. The main character wishes to identify more with the werewolf side rather than the human side, but that wasn't always the case. My gay and transgender friends influenced the main character. While researching Anoka, I came across the "1991 Halloween Blizzard" which tore through several Midwest states on that Halloween night. According to Minnesota's government website, Anoka received the most snowfall, almost thirty inches! I felt compelled to include that in a story. Why not this one? It's also a story of not experiencing the best childhood and wanting nothing but to recreate it as an adult. The main character never had the chance to partake in the awe-someness of Halloween festivities and feels a belonging to this collective. Trying to belong to something new doesn't always work out as planned.

ACKNOWLEDGMENTS

The person who I have to thank first and foremost is my amazing fiancée, Victoria Fletcher. I dedicated this collection to her. She stuck by my side through my dark times and inspired me to keep pushing and achieve whatever that meant. A better lifelong companion, I could not ask for. She is my heart and soul.

My parents have also been there for me through the thick and thin. Both my mom and dad have read everything I've sent their way, and I couldn't be more appreciative. My dad is a full-blooded Native enrolled in the Cheyenne and Arapaho Tribes of Oklahoma and inspired much of what I write as this book is, above all, from an Indigenous perspective. My mom has really helped my writing because, thankfully, she isn't afraid to tell me when something doesn't work, when something needs revision. Throughout this process, she was always excited to read and comment on the next story I would write.

The HOWL Society (Horror-Obsessed Writing and Literature Society) is a horror book club, and soon to be much more, that I joined as a contributing member. It's chock-full of amazing people ready to discuss horror-related anything. There are over a thousand members in its Discord server, however, a great handful of people are always active and there to help with whatever query someone may have. The HOWL Society came together to produce a horror anthology titled *Howls From Hell* which was released May 18, 2021. It features my story, *She's Taken Away*. Our original plan was to release it during StokerCon 2021 and give away paperback copies at a booth, but due to COVID-19, the event is virtual only. This group is an immense inspiration, and the amount of charisma and excitement seeping from its pores helped push me to finish this collection.

During my writing sessions, I often listened to music, sometimes to set the mood and sometimes to drown out any background noise for concentration. Some bands I listened to included: The Dangerous Summer, Hail The Sun, Balance and Composure, Can't Swim, Pianos Become The Teeth, Saosin, Movements, Post Malone, Underøath, and Commonwealth.

My friends deserve a shoutout because they put up with my eagerness throughout 2020 in asking them to be beta readers for some of my stories. I also put some of their personalities into these pages. Thanks and praise to the following friends in alphabetical order so no one gets mad: Aziel Estrada, James Garcia, Stefanie Jones, Jonalyn Lerum, Andrea Mendoza, Patrick Murphy, Marcy Ruiz, Aaron Simeno, Joei Smith, and Ronaldo Velasquez.

There are too many writers out there to list, but so many inspired me to both read and try my hand at writing fiction. Foremost, thank you Stephen Graham Jones for all that you do. For those who don't know, SGJ is a super-talented horror writer who also happens to be of the Blackfeet nation. In fact, he just reached *"New York Times* Bestselling" status for his amazing novel *The Only Good Indians.* His work is stupendous, and he is the main inspiration for putting my wild ideas to paper. Other writers deserving of praise and thanks include Tommy Orange, David Heska Wanbli Weiden, Theodore C. Van Alst, Jr., Grady Hendrix, Rebecca Roanhorse, Gabino Iglesias, Darcie Little Badger, Brian Evenson, Michael Wehunt, Cherie Dimaline, Matthew M. Bartlett, Alex Wolfgang, Kealan Patrick Burke, Jon Padgett, Solomon Forse, Nick Cutter, Duncan Ralston, Victor LaValle, Nathan Ballingrud, Philip K. Dick, and Ray Bradbury.

My stepfather, William F. Stone, passed away in late 2016. He was in my life for sixteen years and for much of it we had a complicated, abrasive relationship. He saw me through all of my dark times, all those years I experienced back-breaking depression, but didn't really get to see how I fought and grew out of that to reach where I am today. He didn't get to smile and feel proud at my college graduation ceremony. He didn't get to applaud my teaching credential. He isn't here to congratulate me on this collection of stories. He won't be there for any other achievements. We all lose loved ones and deal with it in our own varying ways. I'll just have to believe that he would be proud if he were still here. Rest In Peace, Will. I love you, too.

# ABOUT THE AUTHOR

Shane Hawk debuted with the Indigenous horror collection, *Anoka*, in October 2020 and signed with CookeMcDermid Literary Management three months later. In 2023, Penguin Random House will publish *Never Whistle At Night,* an Indigenous dark fiction anthology he's co-editing with Ted Van Alst. When he's not working with students or writing fiction, he enjoys hiking trails, taking photos, making music, and watching classic '80s movies—all with his fiancée, Victoria Fletcher.

Sign up at: shanehawk.com/newsletter

Made in the USA
Monee, IL
04 January 2023